Flowers for the Protestants

Also by Janis Spehr and published by Ginninderra Press
Leaving Ray
Sea Pictures
Ladies, a Plate Please

Janis Spehr

Flowers for the Protestants

– for all my dear friends in Jancourt

Flowers for the Protestants
ISBN 978 1 76041 713 0
Copyright © Janis Spehr 2019
Cover photo: Binyamin Mellish, via Stocksnap

First published 2019 by
GINNINDERRA PRESS
PO Box 3461 Port Adelaide 5015
www.ginninderrapress.com.au

Contents

Flowers for the Protestants

There is no more matriarchal image then the Christian mother of God, who bore a child without male assistance.

Marina Warner, *Alone of All Her Sex: The Myth and the Cult of the Virgin Mary*

Lee sat on the front steps of the Majestic, the big white nineteenth-century honeycomb built to accommodate the overflow from the squatters' weekend parties. She turned the card over and over in her hands, as though asking it a question but the serene-faced Virgin had eyes only for her Son. Last-minute shoppers to and froed along the street in front of the hotel and a teenage girl went by almost dwarfed by a giant toy panda. Lee held the card and her eyes dived into the floating blue-green vista of a late medieval landscape then feasted on the velvet dresses of the two women she supposed were saints. One extended a white lily to the Virgin while the other held the hand of the nestling Infant. Behind them, red roses bloomed, scarlet exclamation points in a hedge of leaves. Who were the women kneeling in the foreground? Probably the wife and daughter of the man who had commissioned the painting: rich bitches wanting their own slice of heaven. She tucked the card into the back pocket of her jeans – the one which didn't contain the photograph – picked up her bag and entered the foyer through the old-fashioned frosted-glass doors.

The same frazzle-permed woman who had worked in the Majestic during the years Lee had spent Saturday nights dancing to Ramones and Talking Heads covers took her money. 'I'll put you in the west wing, love, so the men don't wake you in the morning.'

'Thanks.'

'The men get up at seven, then they don't come back till five.'

'Fine.'

These days, the Majestic was the favourite stopover for road gangs and telecommunications technicians travelling between towns; its public bar was known as the Spew Room. Nothing much had changed, thought Lee, as she climbed the stairs to the residential wing, looking at the faded fleur-de-lis of the carpet through which white cotton cord showed like bone. She hung her clothes in the cupboard and remembered all the times she had come here as a kid, weaving through the trousered legs while her mother waited in the car. Couldn't stand the shame, although the whole town knew, had known for years.

She went to the bathroom at the end of the corridor and stood under the shower, wishing it would sluice away the childhood memories of late-night arguments overheard as she lay rigid in bed. She wished it would drown the screaming and tears of yesterday morning's fight. She saw the sticker as she was towelling her hair dry. 'Ring Gayline…' then the appropriate hours on Wednesday night. It had been graffitied over and someone had tried to rip it off but it remained stubbornly adhering to the tiles. So some things *had* changed: Lee grinned and felt a momentary lift in her spirits as she pulled on her clothes and went downstairs.

'Looks like we're in for a storm,' the woman at the desk called and out on the street great swathes of wind swooped down and chopped the sunlight to short erratic shards.

The sky had a shiny polished look. The birds-of-paradise, brought on the drive down from the city, lay on the passenger side of the car, spiky orange and purple heads pointing towards the big bruise-coloured clouds which had gathered in the west.

Lee drove through the town looking out for people she had gone to school with, or her mother's friends. She had whole conversations stored in her head for the occasions when she met them, lines of script which issued automatically from her mouth in response to questions or inquiries. Ugly red and green decorations hung from the street lights and the shops glowed with the promises of bargains, peace and goodwill.

When she reached the hospital car park, she gathered up the

flowers and crossed to the reception area where white-uniformed women stood chatting beneath a picture of the Sacred Heart. Nice touch, Lee thought, when she saw someone had draped it with a strand of tinsel. One of the nurses recognised her from a previous visit and led her along a glassed-in corridor which connected the new wing of the hospital to the old. The glass was opaque, smoky-grey, and made Lee feel as though she was walking underwater. They took the lift to the second floor.

'How is she?'

'She mainly sleeps now,' the nurse replied. 'She gets restless when the drugs wear off, so we've put her in here.' She gestured in the direction of the room, then went off down the corridor.

Lee lay the birds-of-paradise down next to the ridge of her mother's body. Her face, she thought, it's all beak and bones now. She heard the hiss of the lungs, the two tired old concertinas, and saw the small raised whorls of darns and patches on a sheet made silk-fine by washing.

'Mum,' she whispered, and the grey eyelids fluttered, fragile as moth wings.

'Lee.' Her mother struggled up onto the pillows. 'Have you been here long?'

'Not long. How are you?'

'Lousy. Damn doctors don't know anything.'

'Just rest, Mum. Genevieve sends her love.' Lee indicated the flowers. 'I've brought you these.'

'Oh, yes…yes.' Her mother's eyes focused briefly. 'They're very showy, aren't they?'

'I'll get someone to put them in water.'

'Finding a vase might be difficult. They're a bit out of the ordinary, aren't they?'

'They're tall, that's all. Have you been able to eat anything?'

But her mother was already slipping back to that place where she spent more and more time. Lee patted the sheet. She thought about the photograph nestling in the back pocket of her jeans and wondered what her mother would say, but it was too late for that, too late for everything.

'Just rest, Mum. They're doing all they can. This is the best hospital.'

Her mother turned her head on the pillow and looked through the window, past Lee. 'Catholics,' she said faintly. 'What would they know?'

Out in the car park the hot wind flicked pieces of grit against Lee's calves and the clouds looked as though they would touch the ground. She took the card out of her pocket and propped it against the Land Cruiser's dash. She looked at the scarlet roses. She should have known about the flowers – she had known. It had been a perverse impulse at the florist's to choose something exotic and flashy rather than carnations or lilies or irises. Lee thought about the parade of doctors, the six months of drugs and tubes. She had lied about Genevieve's good wishes.

'So you're going down to visit the old girl? Give her my best, won't you?'

'I will. I'll give her your best bunch of fives and best stream of invective.'

This had been a couple of days ago, before the fight, when they had been joking, as they always did, about Marion's thin-lipped denial. Lee sometimes thought this ability to take the piss was the glue which had kept them together for fifteen years. They had met at the beginning of second-year uni, when a group of GaySoc dykes had balanced a cupboard precariously in a ute tray and driven around the campus, periodically opening the cupboard doors and screaming, 'Here come the lesbians!' to the collective bemusement of straight socialists and footy-playing yobs. Until quite recently, she and Genevieve had been quite capable of attending barbecues at various freshly renovated houses and afterwards screaming with laughter as they recalled earnest discussions about ceiling cornices. But all that had changed: Lee remembered the photograph in her pocket. She glanced at the card again. When they had met, she had been a gauche country girl and Genevieve the recipient of an expensive convent education. Genevieve had taught her to see, had taken her to art galleries and explained the icons and symbols which were the foundation of their culture: how a wall around a group of women meant chastity and inviolability, how a certain flower translated as purity and another as sensuality.

She talked about the historical layers buried beneath the images. 'She's just an inverted fertility goddess,' pointing to the Virgin in a fifteenth-century Annunciation.

'Yeah? Who tipped her upside down?'

Lee turned off a highway down a side road. The hay-making season had recently finished and on either side the paddocks were a chequerboard of blonde stubble and longer grass.

ROAD NARROWS flashed a sign as the asphalt gave way to gravel track. It certainly does, thought Lee grimly. She carried a network of roads in her head, a legacy from summers of aimless teenage driving when she had roamed the countryside, lonely and confused. Once, her whole life had been contained by this web of dirt. The gravel gave way to packed yellow mud and from the top of the rise in front of the house she saw her brother turning out a pen of yearlings. Smoke rose in a bluish cloud behind the line of trees across the paddock and the dogs ran alongside her car, yapping excitedly and making her laugh.

'Neil.'

'Eel.' The old childhood rhyming name.

'Been drenching?'

'Worming.' He leant against the top rail of the fence and took out his rolling tobacco. 'Want one?'

'Ta.' Lee extracted papers and tobacco. Smoke from the line of trees gusted suddenly towards them.

'Well, it's that time of the year. Old Dinny Jackson's burning off.'

'Yeah, mad old bastard. Don't know what good he thinks he does, setting fire to the bush each year.'

'It's a classic case of nature versus culture.' Lee flicked her match into a nearby trough. 'How's everyone?'

'Okay. How's Gen?'

'Fine. She sends her love.' Now would be a good time to tell him, said a little voice in Lee's head. She leant against the fence and watched him suck down smoke. Lines fanned at the corners of his eyes. You poor bastard, she thought suddenly. Neil had been sixteen when he took over the farm, after their father left for good.

He saw her watching and grinned. 'Hey, remember in primary school, we were doing the Christmas story. I was one of the Three Wise Men...'

'...and you nearly wrecked everything by singing the wrong words to "We Three Kings of Orient Are". How did they go?' and laughing, they sang,

> 'We Three Kings of Orient are
> One on a tractor, one in a car
> One on a scooter blowing a hooter
> Following yonder star...'

'Arsehole,' said Lee. 'I thought you'd be expelled, or failed for the year.'

'Come on,' he said, flicking his butt onto the concrete. 'Let's go inside.'

As they crossed the yard, they saw the cows huddled in a corner of the paddock, their backs against the wind. The air felt tense, as though someone held their fist against the sky and was pushing it out.

'Wipe your boots, please!' Marlene stood at the sink mixing batter.

She had lost weight since Lee's last visit and had dyed her dull blonde hair a shade of red which, Lee saw with satisfaction, made her look like tough old mutton dressed as lamb. Pieces of dried fruit slid round and round the bowl, large and dark as eyes.

'Hi.'

'Hi.' Lee put the sack of presents on the table as her nephews streamed into the kitchen.

'Auntie Lee! Auntie Lee!' Phillip, the younger and Lee's sweetie, threw his arms around her. 'Presents, Auntie Lee? Presents?'

'Not yet, mate. You can open them in a couple of days.' Lee swung him onto her knee.

From the corner of her eye, she caught Marlene's expression. You fat-arsed moll, Lee thought viciously. She imagined showing the photograph to Marlene and Marlene's comments later to a friend on the phone: 'It's not normal, is it? It's not normal but then what would you expect?'

Neil took down mugs and poured hot water over instant coffee as the boys raced off, distracted by something on television. Now would be the time, the little voice in Lee's head urged. Now would be as good a time as any. Her gaze snagged on the ugly tinsel tree propped in the lounge room and she took a mouthful of coffee which was terrible as usual, too weak and too milky.

'Down here long?' Marlene pulled out a chair from the table.

'Just for a few days.' Lee reached for a ginger nut and let herself be carried along by the flow of small talk. Sitting here was always familiar but alien; she contrasted the smooth wood and glossy painted cupboards with the clutter of her childhood. Marlene had demanded a new kitchen as a wedding present and all the old furniture and skulking piles of paper had been thrown out. Lee remembered Marlene in the playground at primary school, organising the other little girls; when she had set her sights on Neil, he hadn't stood a chance.

She took another mouthful of coffee. 'We need to talk about Mum.'

'Yeah.' Her brother toyed with his mug. 'How is she?'

'Out of it.' Lee glanced at him sharply. 'Haven't you seen her?'

'We went in last week. She looked crook.'

'She is crook. She's dying.'

'You don't know that.' He looked down at the table and frowned.

'You think she's getting better?'

'I don't know…maybe the change in hospitals…the Micks might be able to help her out…'

'No one can "help her out".' Lee raised her voice. She's only going to get worse!'

'You don't know that…'

'Oh, get your head out of the sand! We need to make arrangements…'

'Neil's been arranging things for a while now. We both have.' Marlene cut in smoothly, as though speaking to a recalcitrant child.

Lee put down her mug carefully and looked at them. She knew the subtext here. He stayed home when you went off to uni. He put up with Marion's whingeing and tantrums when you were putting up posters and making a nuisance of yourself. He held things together while you were being a big-shot lawyer in the city. You come back here and think you're better than us, you deviant, deviant, deviant.

She stood up and pushed in her chair with trembling hands. 'This doesn't seem to be the best time and I have to get back to the hospital. We'll talk about things before I go. Thanks for the cuppa.'

Outside, the wind rattled the leaves of the nectarine tree and flattened the white tufts of grass. It felt as though the whole world was holding its breath. Coward, said the little voice, as Lee drove down the track. You really are a coward. Lee pressed her fingers to the throb incubating in her right temple. 'Just tell them!' Genevieve had screamed yesterday morning. 'Who gives a fuck what they think!'

Lee pressed her other temple while overhead the sky hovered like a reluctant benediction and white fingers of static snaked their way through the old T-Rex song on the radio. She glanced at the dash and saw the card. Shit. She had forgotten to give it to them. She jammed it into the pocket which held the photograph. I should throw them both away, she thought, that would be the easiest solution…

'Cocksucker! Red neck!'

If it hadn't been for the shouting, Lee wouldn't have noticed them at the traffic lights. The thin dark one held the pale chubby one with one hand and gave the finger to a passing yob to the other.

Go, girls, thought Lee and waved as she went past but it didn't help her headache and by the time she reached the hospital dark spikes of pain thrust at the base of her skull. Her mother lay propped against pillows, shoulders draped with fuzzy wool. A vase of glowing, open-throated pink and gold roses stood on the top of the metal cabinet beside the bed. At Lee's touch, her eyes jerked open.

'Do you want me to help you with that?'

'Oh, don't bother about it.'

'It's no bother. Here.' Lee took a long bone strung with pouches of flesh and threaded it into the sleeve. When she walked around to the other side of the bed, she looked down into the garden below and saw the two black-robed figures moving slowly along the rows of blooms, snipping and picking. 'Who are they?' She walked over to the window.

'What? Oh, they're just two old nuns. Retired. They still wear the old habit. Too old to change.'

'It's a habit they can't get out of,' Lee suggested.

'Her mother laughed weakly. 'They're just kept on to walk around and pick a bunch of flowers for the Protestants. They gave me these.' She pointed to the roses.

'Oh, beautiful.' Lee touched a petal which was soft as a young girl's skin. She buried her face in the heavy, old-fashioned perfume then gently clasped her mother's arm. Darkness pressed in at the corners of the windows.

'Those tough old Irish nuns,' murmured her mother. 'Good people, I suppose…good people, in their own way…although you do feel sorry for them.'

'Yeah? Picking flowers for the Protestants looks like an easy life to me.' Lee reached for the empty sleeve.

'Well…no husband…no family…no love…'

For a moment, black light clouded Lee's eyes and the sleeve slipped from her hand. She wanted to rip the old arm out of its socket, hear the bones splinter and crack and leave the whole bloody mess for someone else to clean up. It was over in an instant; she slid the arm in smoothly and carefully set it down.

'There's different kinds of families,' she said but her voice sounded hollow and thin. 'Different kinds of love.'

'Oh, yes,' murmured her mother drowsily.

The two figures walked slowly up the path which led away from the garden, halted for a moment at the gate in the wall then disappeared.

'Good people…in their own way.'

Lee patted the sheet and drew up the blankets. On the shelf above the bed stood the birds-of-paradise, stems jammed into utilitarian glass. The lamplight threw their spiky heads against the walls and the shadows looked like fingers, a clutch of questing hands.

An hour later, in the lounge bar of the Majestic, things seemed a little better.

'I heard about your mum.' The woman behind the bar shovelled ice into Lee's glass. 'She's a real old battler, a real old sweetheart.'

A real old sweetheart! How Marion would hate being described like that! Lee set down her third Scotch and contemplated the table of teenagers nearby, the boys clowning to make the chicks laugh while the jukebox thrashed away in the background. She had sometimes been part of groups like that when she was their age but she had never felt comfortable, had always known she was faking it.

Lee swilled a mouthful of Scotch which tasted medicinal. She rarely drank: during the summers she had spent driving the back roads, beer or cans of cheap mixer drinks had been her constant companions. 'It's a wonder I didn't run the car up a bloody tree,' she told Genevieve years later, and it seemed part of her always remained that frightened adolescent, ready to cauterise some residual guilt and shame with alcohol. When she learned how easy it was to crawl inside a bottle, she had understood some things about her family. She thought about the old body lying in the hospital: Marion's kindness had been dried from her, her life had become a stubborn battle to maintain her family's dignity and pride. You were stronger than her was, thought Lee, and you never let him forget it.

She drained her glass and was about to leave when the door opened and in they came, the thin dark one holding the pale chubby one by the hand. They ignored the stares and comments and went up to the bar. On their way to a vacant table, they had to pass the group of kids. Lee didn't hear what was said but she saw the pale chubby one draw back as though she had been struck and the thin dark one swing around to a blonde boy with matted hair and rough skin.

'You talkin' to us, shithead?"

'Oh, piss off, you leso slut.' The boy had already turned away when the surge of beer caught him on the side of his face. He swore again and lunged, but the man who managed the Majestic was quicker.

'All right, you two, get out! Go on, outside!'

Outside, the cars in the street had their lights on and Lee caught the girls up as they stood at the corner, still holding hands.

'That was unfair,' she said.

'Shit happens.' The pale chubby one shrugged. 'That fuckhead's hassled us before.'

The wind ballooned the moments of silence which followed.

Lee shifted from one foot to the other. 'You're brave.'

The thin dark one made an obscene farting noise. 'What's there to be brave about? You want to do Macca's? KFC?'

'Nah,' said Lee. 'It's all arseholes and crumbs, isn't it?'

'Yeah, just like men.' The pale chubby one looked at her. 'You can come back to our place. We've got a bottle of Southern.'

'Our place' was a flat tacked onto an ugly brick veneer and pinched against the back fence. There was a scarred coffee table and a motley assortment of chairs which said St Vinnies. Lee sank into a green vinyl beanbag and thought wistfully of the cream, high-ceilinged rooms she had left behind yesterday.

'S'er mum's place.' The think dark one jerked a thumb towards the other. 'She's Lyssa, I'm Kyle.'

'Lee.'

'Yo, Lee.'

Kyle poured from the bottle of Southern Comfort then filled the glasses with Coke. She handed one to Lee, who took a cautious mouthful and almost gagged; the drink tasted like liquid jelly beans.

'Cheers.'

'Yeah, cheers.' Kyle pulled up a worn armchair while Lyssa moved about shutting windows as the first thunder sounded outside. 'So, what brings you to this thriving metropolis?'

'My mother's in the hospital.'

'Yeah? What's wrong with her?'

Lee held up curved thumb and forefinger.

'The big C?'

'Yeah.'

'She's gunna die?'

'Yeah.'

'Oh.' Kyle considered her drink for a moment. 'What about ya dad?'

'Ratbag,' said Lee. 'Boozer. Went up north when I was fifteen and I never saw him again.' What had it been about Harry? She didn't know; something putrid in the blood.

'Got any brothers and sisters?'

'Jesus, Kyle, give it a rest.' Lyssa's voice was already blurry at the edges. The command came out sounding almost maternal.

'I was just askin'!'

'That's all right,' said Lee. She downed the rest of her drink as another wave of thunder rolled across the sky. 'Seeing we're on the subject of families...' She reached into her pocket and threw the photograph on the table. 'What do you make of that?'

'It's a worm!'

'It's a germ!'

'Is it yours?' asked Kyle.

'My girlfriend's,' said Lee.

'Yeah?' Kyle picked up the photograph. 'It's awesome.'

'So you say.'

'Don't you want it?' Lyssa looked at Lee sadly.

'I don't know.' Lee felt the familiar surge of helplessness. 'She wanted one...it seemed like a good idea...we've been together a long time...'

'Where'dja get the stuff?'

'What stuff?'

'You know...' Kyle pointed to her crotch. 'The stuff.'

'Oh. A poofta friend of ours.'

Lee tilted her head back. It had taken a month to persuade Greg and even then he had made sour comments about stud bulls. 'They're happy enough to spread it around when they don't have to think about the consequences,' Genevieve had remarked wryly after an abortive meeting. *We were too hard on him,* thought Lee. *He wanted to help, just got caught up in the rush of responsibility none of us anticipated.* She opened her eyes to find Kyle's gaze locked on hers.

'Not gunna leave her holdin' the baby, are ya?'

'You're very perceptive for a young person.' Lee tried for a grin but it slid greasily off her face. When she had stopped off at the florists that morning, she had also gone to the newsagent. She had bought several maps then sat in the car, her eyes tracing rivers and the branching red arteries of roads. She had smelt frangipani and felt warm breezes caress her skin. Now she just felt old and tired. The thunder sounded huge as cathedrals at the window. 'What do you think I should do?'

Kyle looked at her silently over the top of the glass. In the dim yellowish light, her eyes gleamed wetly as a wild animal's. 'I think ya should try to be happy.'

'Happy?'

'Yeah.' Lyssa reached for the bottle. 'What do you want?'

'What do I want?'

'Is there an echo in here? Hello! Hello!' Kyle cupped her hands around her mouth.

A pistol crack of lightning made them all jump.

Kyle looked at Lee again. 'You're afraid, aren't ya? Afraid you'll stuff it up like your own olds did?'

'I suppose so,' Lee said.

She and Neil had got used to the unlikely places they would come across stashes of bottles and cans and of Harry's sudden unexplained absences. 'Dad must have a bit of abo in him,' Neil had said to her once. 'All the walkabouts he takes.'

Lee refilled her glass and felt the room tilt alarmingly. 'I don't know... I don't know whether I'd be any good with kids.'

'Ya talkin' to us, aren't ya? We're young enough ta be ya kids.'

Lee laughed. She took a large slug from her drink. 'It'll look a bit funny, though…look a bit funny in the family Bible.'

Kyle let out one of her farting noises.

'We make our own families,' said Lyssa, starting to roll a joint with small capable peasant's hands.

'Yeah, yeah,' said Lee.

She had heard it all before: from her friends, in gay magazines and newspapers and at the Lesbian Parenting Conference. She had been surprised at the number of women there. They had brought their anger and frustration but also their hope. 'We're treated like pariahs,' the spokeswoman at the plenary session had said, 'told we're not real women, that we're child molesters and unfit to mother. Well, all that has to change.' There had been endless discussions and many agendas, practical plans and wild ideas, as they struggled to break the bond between culture and genetics. The whole weight of their history and tradition told them what they were doing was wrong, all their awkwardly spliced connections cutting across the laws of family, God and those clean unbroken lines of descent. It had moved Lee and disturbed her, this talk of test tubes and tribes, of full moon conceptions and appropriate male role models; it seemed to her that the dense tangles of blood and kin could not so easily be unravelled. She had left early; there had been another row with Genevieve, whose face held all the certainty Lee now saw in the girl sitting across from her.

'Don'tcha think ya all right?' Kyle asked fiercely. 'Don'tcha think ya a good person?'

'Yes,' said Lee weakly, answering the question she had been asking herself for years while all the time the old awful mantra *not good enough, not good enough* droned in her head. 'I'm just worried I'll pass on the bad things…'

'Why? Do ya think you'll only pass on bad things?'

'No, of course not…'

'Well, then, there ya fucken go.' Kyle slumped in a satisfied heap and took the joint which Lyssa handed her. She passed it to Lee, who shook her head.

'That stuff doesn't agree with me.'

'It doesn't agree with me either but I still smoke it.' Kyle ran a hand through her hair, spiking it wildly against her scalp. Sweat and alcohol lacquered her skin and Lee glimpsed a subterranean violence she knew she should treat with care.

The room shifted hazily; she tried focusing but everything blurred. She set down her glass heavily and some of the liquid ran down the sides and congealed on the table. There was something lying there and it seemed vaguely familiar: the last thing Lee saw as she passed out was the velvety sheen of the dresses swimming up to meet her.

When she woke she was lying on the floor, covered with a blanket, and the rained had started. Great warm drops anointed her face as she staggered out to the front lawn and threw up. She stood there gasping and trying to get her bearings while the rain stuck her shirt of her skin and rat-tailed her hair. The houses which lined the street were as ugly as the one behind her. Lee shuddered and went back inside to the stink of grog and empty bottles. She picked up a smeared glass, filled it from the tap, drank, refilled it and drank again while she tried to order her wretched trembling brain.

Lyssa and Kyle lay clasped together under another blanket. Lyssa's face was flushed, her mouth was open and she snored softly, while Kyle still had her leather vest on; Lee caught a glimpse of the unicorn inkily etched on one small breast. She held the glass and stared at the sleeping girls. She hadn't asked them anything about their lives, knew nothing about them. Were they sixteen? Seventeen? *Young enough to be ya kids.* A school bag lay in one corner of the room, with a pile of dirty clothes next to it. I had to invent myself, Lee thought, but it hasn't been quite so hard for them. They walk through this squalid little town holding hands. What's there to be brave about? And perhaps she had had something to do with it. Perhaps all the posters and speeches of her young years amounted to something, after all. It seemed a dubious genealogy. She picked up the photograph then saw the card which had been accidentally pulled out with it. It had been used as a coaster, was dog-eared and the Virgin's face stained brown. Lee quelled her heaving stomach and stared at the group of women surrounding the Child and suddenly she saw beyond the perfection of the image to an alternate vision.

'You had your own problems, didn't you, what with the kid having a surrogate father and then choosing such a strange career path?' she murmured. 'Yet you seemed to manage.'

She glanced across at the young women. I've spent all my life chasing an unobtainable ideal, she thought, trying to compensate, blaming myself. It's taken them to show me that there are rarely safe gardens. We make our own families. She considered scrawling a flippant thank you and leaving the card for them – no, she'd send them something they'd appreciate. Lee picked it up: the light gleamed off the gold edging the women's robes, and glinted on the crown two cherubs held above the Virgin's head. The image enshrined a passive femininity she had rejected all her life but it seemed to her it also held a residual splendour, some lost power which looked either backwards or forwards. She pushed the card into her pocket together with the photograph, then looked at her watch. It was ten past six on Christmas Eve morning. She closed the door quietly behind her.

Out on the street the rain fell in streams across her face and she had a sudden vision of it raining and raining until the water carried the topsoil away and beat the flowers and shrubs into sodden vegetable submission. Lee closed her eyes and momentarily her head seethed with images of drains running pustulant yellow-green and bloated animal carcasses turning over and over. She shook her head and the air smelt like water again. By the time she reached the Majestic, she was soaked.

'Hard night?' the woman who worked on the reception desk asked sympathetically. She towed a small trolley behind her which held plastic buckets, bottles of various cleaning fluids and a bright orange duster.

Lee raised her hand in greeting, climbed the stairs and forced her body under the shower. Clouds of steam billowed around her as she turned on the water so hard the blood rose beneath the surface of her skin and she swayed and shook. When she finished, she leaned against the tiles, dizzy and dehydrated, and wondered whether she was doing the right thing. *Not gunna leave her holdin' the baby, are ya?* Her face in the mirror looked hollow-eyed and hungover and she grimaced and stuck out her tongue. On her way out, she glanced at the sticker, peeling slightly but still hanging on, and she gave it an affectionate flick with her towel.

Lee threw her things into her bag and went downstairs. Great glittering stretches of water lay at the sides of the road and silver arcs flew up from the Land Cruiser's wheels. Momentarily a curve of light coloured like parrot feathers stretched above her then vanished, leaving a bluish-green sky with membranes of cloud at the horizon. The town was soon behind her; she drove past the turn-off to her brother's farm and glanced down the road without slowing. There's different kinds of families, different kinds of love. Lee laughed and sounded the horn.

When she reached the next small town, she stopped at its only florist. 'I'll take all your roses,' said Lee, handing her a credit card.

'Oh, beautiful, beautiful,' the woman kept repeating like an incantation as she lifted long-stemmed bunch after bunch into the car.

They filled the back of the Land Cruiser: red, white, salmon pink, yellow and mauve, and Lee wished there were more, enough to make one room of the house into a soft, petal-filled cavern. She was singing as she drove off, some corny old song she remembered from years ago, 'I beg your pardon, I never promised you a rose garden…'

It was true: there were no guarantees to happiness. We fall from grace and are forever outside the Garden but we do the best we can. Shit happens, but we go on and connections can be lost and broken or nourished and held. As the road flattened out before her, she passed a house with a young pine tree growing at the gateway, a living tree coming straight from the ground which someone had decked with spangles and a star. Lee laughed and sounded her horn. There was no certainty, only possibility. She'd work something out; she'd give it a go. She had the card and the photograph side by side on the dash, the glowing reds and greens of the Flemish painting and the grey smudges of the ultrasound; and they looked all right together.

Mushrooming

Two girls and their mother went mushrooming.

'Come on, we'll go down the back paddock,' said the mother, placing the knives in the bottom of the baskets.

It was May and the air was damp and carried the smell of wood smoke. It caused the elder girl to fill with a certain melancholy happiness; she was twelve now and things often made her shiver. She picked up one of the baskets and ploughed through the slurry of mud and chook shit in the front yard.

'Come on, Sammie.' She held up one strand of the barbed wire fence so that her sister could scramble through. 'Hey, wait a minute!'

Sammie was running on down the paddock, her mind on the mushrooms with their dark frilled underskirts and stems which snapped like chalk. She was like that, heedless. She often had to be told to do things properly. When her sister called, she turned back reluctantly and helped her through the fence.

Their mother came out of the house, wearing overalls and carrying the other basket. 'The one who finds the most mushrooms doesn't have to do the dishes tonight,' she sang out after them.

They started working their way around the back paddock, eyes trawling through dense patches of clover and tussocks of rye grass. The elder girl knew where to look, near the ossified grey patties of cow shit, but Sammie was quicker and didn't have to carry a basket.

'Found some!' she shouted.

'Don't be stupid,' said the elder girl. 'You can't eat them,' and she kicked at the clustered toadstools, with their pale, brown-spotted hoods and drooping gills. They gave way before her boot with a rotten tearing sound and pieces of yellow fungus flew through the air. But where they landed there were real mushrooms, birthed from the black soil by the recent rain.

'They're mine!' the elder girl called as Sammie started towards them.

They reached the mushrooms together but as they bent down with the knives Sammie said, 'I'll tell on you. I'll tell Mum what I saw you doing.'

The elder girl stood still as stone, staring into her sister's round blue eyes.

'I saw you,' Sammie said. 'You and Bernie MacGuire.' And she started to cut the mushrooms, dropping the dark fragrant weight of them into the red woollen hat she had taken off. 'I'm going to put mine in here,' she said.

The elder sister looked at her for a moment then walked away. There was complete silence except for a magpie carolling and off in the distance, the dull thud of an axe against wood. A small clot of cloud had torn itself free from the larger mass and floated overhead, pinkish-mauve against grey. The elder sister kept her eyes on the ground and her thoughts to herself. She found some mushrooms which were just small white knobs pushing out of the earth and others big as bread and butter plates and left a trail of black spores behind them as she severed their stems. Sammie was over the other side of the paddock, close to her mother and every now and then the elder girl saw them bend and cut.

'My hat's full,' Sammie shouted after a while and she held it up for them to see.

'Good girl, you clever thing,' their mother said. 'Come on, we'll do one more paddock, then we'll go home.'

The elder sister walked to the fence and waited for Sammie.

'I'll tell on you,' Sammie said, as she wriggled through. 'You had your pants down.'

The elder girl said nothing, just waited until her mother and Sammie were far ahead, searching under the trees where the cows sheltered in rough weather. She stuck to the outside of the paddock, alongside the fence, and didn't find any more.

'We'll go home,' called the mother at last. 'Come on, kids.'

'I'll race you,' said Sammie, looking into the elder sister's almost empty basket and she scuttled ahead, like one of the little bugs, thought her sister, which run out from under the cow pats.

They were neck and neck at the first fence, with their mother bringing up the rear, calling encouragement to first one, then the other. They clambered through the fence, which snagged their jumpers and tore at their hair. The basket clunked against the elder sister's side and she fought for breath as they ran up the rise to the second fence. Her body had started to thicken; there were clothes she couldn't fit into any more.

'Come on,' she said, holding up the wire. 'That's enough. I'll help you through.' She put her boot on the bottom strand, pressing it down, and waited for her sister. When Sammie was halfway through, the elder sister bent down and gently squeezed the small white fingers around the barb. She thought she almost heard a soft 'pop' as it pierced the tender flesh.

'Mum!' screamed Sammie, looking down at the ribbon of blood. 'Mum!'

But the mother was out of sight, still coming up the rise.

'Don't you say anything,' the elder sister said. 'Don't you say anything.'

She breathed deeply, inhaling the incense of wood smoke, and thought about the fire around which the family would sit that evening. There would be long black logs which the flames ate, charring the undersides scarlet, and which, when struck, ignited a shower of sparks, bright as metal.

The Red Jumper

He was standing by the cash register when she came into the shop, a wiry little piece with blonde hair he doubted was natural. She looked all right, though, didn't have any rings through her nose or green plaits.

'You right there, are you? Anything I can help you with?'

And then there was her question about the jumper; the story about running out of petrol that morning and having to walk to the shop.

'Your wife sold me some, even though I didn't have any money.'

She dropped a few coins into his hand. He wasn't surprised. When he'd been out on the farm, he was always pulling bogged cars out of mud or towing the ones which had broken down. Even here, it happened; tourists staying in the big town up the road came out to look at the scenery and got into trouble. Annette would have sold her the petrol in an empty oil container they kept out the back – illegal because it was plastic. The girl would have been flustered, worried about leaving her car and not having any money. That's why she'd forgotten her jumper.

'I'll ask the wife,' and he went out the back, where Annette stood preparing chips.

Skeins of peel curled like dirty ribbons in the sink. When he asked her about the jumper ,her face went blank.

'No, I haven't seen it.'

'You sure? One of the girls might have…'

'No.' She looked at him patiently, the peeler clutched in her hand. 'She's got the wrong end of the stick. She must have left it somewhere else.'

'We haven't seen it, love,' and he watched the pretty face fall in disappointment.

'Oh, well, if you do…'

'Yeah, yeah,' he said, taking the piece of paper with the scribbled phone number. He wanted her out of there; he could see Des the ambo coming along the footpath for a packet of smokes, his beanie pulled down over his ears. Des held the door open for the little blonde and gave her the once over as she went through.

'G'day.'

'G'day, Des.' Automatically he reached for a packet of Peter Jackson and waited while Des ambled around collecting biscuits and dog food.

'Wish he wouldn't come here,' Annette had said, not long ago.

'He only lives around the corner, he's entitled,' he'd answered but she was right, he felt the man's presence like a judgement. It didn't matter how many times Des came in for cigarettes and cans of Pal, he would always see him bent over Damien's body, big hands pressing down and his ear cocked for a sigh of breath. When he saw Des, he smelt dank water and saw green slime.

He gave the man his change and got Annette to take over while he sat in front of the television having his tea and refereeing his daughters. Shouts carried faintly from the oval down the road where the footy team trained under lights; he saw the night air stained white by young men's breath and veils of steam rising in the showers.

Later, the blokes came tramping into the shop, calling out to him with flushed faces and slicked down hair. 'Hey, Graeme, how's it going, mate?' They milled around, ordering drinks and greasy food, reminding him of the time he was their age and had done the same thing. In a few years…but he wouldn't let himself think about it. He shovelled chips into bags and piled slabs of meat onto hamburgers then cleaned up and switched out the lights.

The first thing he saw when he walked into the bedroom was the jumper draped like a flag across the old dresser. Bright red, just as the girl had described. Like the colour of geraniums when they first open. Annette had once had a skirt the same colour, a silky thing which belled softly from her hips. She must have found the jumper when she was tidying up. He'd give the girl a call tomorrow. He piled his clothes neatly onto a chair and eased quietly into bed, even though he knew nothing could wake Annette once the drugs had kicked in. He lay there with his eyes open, listening to the dark.

The sounds were all different in town. He used to get up during the night, after his son died, and stand at the kitchen window, hearing the dry screaming of possums and the wind strumming the antenna on the roof. Under moonlight, the dam was a dark unblinking eye. Dawn always came as a surprise, that first metallic harshness unsoftened by sun and he'd stumble out to the old privy to have a piss and unchain the dogs. He'd get cranky with Annette in the dairy and sometimes, when she left to get the girls off to school, she wouldn't return. He'd come in for morning tea and she'd be at the sink, looking out the window, staring, staring at the dam. He came in one morning to find her with the carving knife resting lazily against one wrist, from which oozed a dark glistening tear.

'A fresh start might do you the world of good,' said the doctor as he wrote out the prescription for the pills. 'Might be just what you need,' and then he told them about the old lady selling up in town.

'Well, it's just a spot on the highway,' Annette said when they went to look it over.

'Yep, just a spot on the highway,' he echoed, and in the end, that's what they called it.

People said that they were mad to buy the shop, that they wouldn't make a go of it, but they'd done all right. It was her idea to put the collection of old bottles and tins in the windows to get the tourists in, the tea tin with the kookaburra on it and the flat metal boxes which had once held cigarettes. He usually spun some bullshit about them all belonging to his grandfather but they were mainly old junk he'd found when he'd cleaned out the sheds on the farm, along with yellowing copies of the *Weekly Times* and rabbit carcasses hung up to dry years ago. They painted the shop cream with dark green trim – 'heritage' colours Annette called them – and he got a sign writer to design a scroll above the door. 'Proprietors: Graeme and Annette Maxwell'. Annette had learned to make biscuits and fudge squares and rum balls which she boxed with gingham covers and sold to the tourists. He tried not to think about the farm but he missed it like a wound, especially in spring when the grass was beginning to kick and the calves lay neat as parcels at their mothers' feet. The dam was out of sight but he still carried Damien with him and at night dream-tentacles wrapped his sleep until he sweated and cried out. He flailed through black water but always his son lay out of reach, arms upturned like a sacrifice and hair a floating film of blonde weed. When his mouth opened to shout Damien's name, water rushed in and his nostrils clogged with dirt. He clutched at flesh and bone which dissolved into white ripples and floated away.

He woke with fragments of the dream still clinging and stumbled down the passage to sluice them off. When he came out of the bathroom, waist wrapped with a towel, Jayne was standing outside the girls' room, her arms overflowing with Princess, the big old tabby they'd kept from the farm.

'This cat smells like kitchens,' she announced gravely.

'Don't be stupid,' he said. 'A cat can't smell like a kitchen,' but later as he spooned down cereal, he sniffed surreptitiously at the old cat's fur and caught bread and cinnamon and his daughter's own warm body scent. He took the broom and stood outside, raising his head to the air like a dog as the chills lifted from the street. The oak trees opposite filtered the rising sun; the chemist a few doors up and the butcher on the other side were getting ready for the day and soon there was a line of brooms going 'swish, swish' in the gentle light.

By the time he finished sweeping, he felt better. He turned the 'Closed' sign to 'Open' and went inside to have the rest of his breakfast.

Annette stood at the sink opening a litre carton of milk. She was wearing the red jumper.

For a moment, he just stood there. Annette had always been a cuddly girl, was a lot larger than the little blonde, and the jumper pulled tightly across her breasts.

'You said you couldn't find it,' he said at last.

'What?' She picked up the kettle and turned on the tap.

'You said you couldn't find it.'

'What are you talking about? Oh, this.' She plucked at the jumper. 'She left it behind yesterday.'

'You told me you didn't know where it was!'

'So?' She looked at him as though he was stupid, turned the tap off and plugged the kettle in. Drops of water beaded the stainless steel then thinned into rivulets down its sides.

'But it's not yours! It doesn't even fit you!'

'It'll stretch,' she said and tugged complacently at the wool.

'What if she comes back and sees you wearing it?'

'She won't – she was a tourist. She started going on about how "quaint" the bottles were. I had to shut her up.'

'I've got her number. I could ring her.'

'Suit yourself.' She shrugged and turned away. 'I'm going to make toast. Do you want one slice or two?'

They had breakfast in silence then she took the car off somewhere while he went into the shop and started stacking shelves. It was a job which always bored him and ordinarily he tried to make a game of it, grouping tins of a certain size or colour on the floor then ranging up and down the aisles placing them where they were meant to go but this morning his legs stayed weighted to the floor.

He stood stolidly bending and stacking until the bell on the door clanged and Des came in for his paper. The bloke looked seedy. Des lived alone, didn't have any company except for his greyhounds and a couple of ferrets. While he was in the ambo's uniform, he looked all right but today he wore old corduroy pants and gave off a sour smell, like mud drying in the sun. Under the fluorescent light, his nose was purple as a baboon's arse.

'I was out at your old place yesterd'y. The wife gets asthma. The grass is up over the fence.'

'Yeah?' They'd sold the place to a TAFE college professor and his wife who wanted to run a few horses. When he showed them around, he could see the wife doing sums in her head, adding up the cost of remodelling the kitchen and putting in a new bathroom. He wasn't surprised to hear that they'd let things go. He'd thought that they'd probably tear the old weatherboard down and build some ugly brick thing big as a space ship with a flat easy care native garden. He stuffed a packet of cheese slices, cigarettes and a copy of *Post* into a plastic bag and handed it to Des, who grunted and looked at him shyly.

'I seen your missus take off this morning like a bat outta hell.'

'Yeah, she's busy.'

He turned back to the shelves, trying to work out where to put some tins of condensed milk, then glanced up to see the man's small grey eyes glazed with pity. Get out, he thought, feeling stripped and flayed. Get out, ripping the top from the carton and not looking up until he heard the bell clang. He tore the box open and wondered where Annette was. She'd got into a habit of going off like this and he didn't feel he could ask her about it. There was a certain privacy she'd always had that he never felt he could impose upon. The skirt she'd owned, the colour of dying autumn leaves, she'd worn it when they first started going together. He'd pick her up in his father's old Holden which usually sat in the shed and they'd drive to the beach, taking the back roads because he was still too young for a licence. They could go a whole afternoon without seeing anyone, just sitting on top of the cliffs watching the sea change colour under the sky or walking along the beach with the fierce tug of water around their ankles. When they first started doing it, they used the Holden's back seat but after a while they got braver and would spread a rug on the harsh tussocky grass which covered the dunes. One evening after they'd finished, they'd walked along the beach and come to a place where the ocean had sucked out scoop of sand and left a trench of water behind, through which fronds of seaweed waved.

It was almost dark when Annette handed him her shirt and stepped into the pool.

'What are you doing?' he'd asked, half frightened, because this wasn't like her, but she just stood there with the darkness brushing her shoulders and the skirt spread and gently floating.

'Hey, come out of there!'

He'd started to wade in but stopped when she held up her hand and it seemed now, as he knelt dazedly among the tins, that he'd caught a glimpse of something buried deep which would either flower or spoil; he'd waited until she stepped from the water. The warm air dried the skirt and left a salty stain along the hem. He wondered what had happened to it, whether it lay at the bottom of one of the boxes they'd never bothered to unpack or whether Annette had sent it to the Salvos long ago.

As they drove back from the beach that evening, with the Holden's headlights picking out startled rabbits on the road, he hadn't known what to say. Perhaps if he had, she wouldn't be sinking into bottomless sleep and he wouldn't be spending his nights sifting bones and silt.

bones

and

silt

His son was just bones and silt now.

When he heard the car pull up, he looked out the window, thinking it must be Annette but it wasn't the station wagon, just some Jap tin can with a dented fender.

The blonde girl got out and he gripped the shelf. She stared both ways along the street and for a moment he thought she was going somewhere else but then she looked through the window straight at him. The chemist's black and white border collie bounded up and she laughed and put out her hand. Now he remembered; she'd said she'd be back – 'just in case it turns up' – when he'd pushed her out the door. It seemed he forgot a lot of things these days, the correct way to put stock on shelves or where a lost garment might be found. She waved to him as she started across and he drew back his lips like a cornered animal.

His mouth opened to form words of promise or denial but the sounds snagged and eddied in his chest and as she came towards him, he smelt the stench of floating carrion and felt the water close over his head.

35

Crossing the Border

The seeds broke through the mangoes like white bone shining through flesh. All that remained when they had finished were the oblong pips covered in fibrous tufts of gold. Juice dripped off their chins and stuck their fingers together. They threw the pips in the bin and washed their hands at the basin in the public toilet block. Behind one of the doors someone had written, 'God loves all sinners, even you.'

'It gives you confidence, doesn't it?' she said.

'It makes me realise we're in Queensland,' Letitia replied.

They drove through a night thick and sticky as molasses dripping off a spoon. From the road, she could see islands of light, and silhouettes talking or preparing food. 'In dreams I walk with you,' sang Roy Orbison, 'in dreams I talk to you.'

'What time do you think we'll arrive?'

'Mid-morning, probably. I told Len we'd be there for lunch.'

She glanced across at the hands gripping the wheel and saw the hairs on the sinewy arms beginning to sprout black. In a few days, Letitia would take out the peroxide and go through the ritual she had been performing every summer since she was fourteen. The peroxide made her skin redden and flake off but she kept it on till the hair shone like burnished copper.

'I don't know why you bother.'

'Huh?' Letitia's brows drew together momentarily before her gaze returned to the moon-slicked road. 'If it bothers you so much, find yourself a nice blue-eyed WASP…like the one before me.'

'Kathy was a bottle blonde too, actually, but she used it on her head, not her arms.'

'Different place, same principle.'

'She'd been brought up on reruns of Marilyn Monroe movies, was hooked on the idea that blondes have more fun.'

'I wouldn't know.'

She dozed intermittently. Once she dreamt she was lying under a canopy of trees with broad, flat leaves. They began to press down, coming closer and closer, until she could put her hand through the thick dark foliage.

When she woke, the radio was hissing static and the sky was changing to the cold steel blue of dawn. They ate breakfast at a café on the outskirts of another nondescript town. She sat a the table watching the men who did the long haul from Sydney to Brisbane talk and joke among themselves. Most of them were red-eyed and bristle-chinned and they all wore singlets, shorts and either thongs or heavy work boots. One had the back view of a naked woman tattooed the length of one arm in swirls of red or blue.

'Do you reckon they ever do it with each other?'

'If they did, I think they'd keep it pretty quiet.'

'It would be the perfect cover, though, wouldn't it? All those blokes on the road, with the little woman and kids safely at home.'

Their grins meshed for a moment. She dipped her finger into the slops caused by the waitress banging down the saucers on the table. A pity to waste two years of art school. A stem. What's the middle bit, the part around which the petals cluster. Stamen? She drew the petals. She loves me, she loves me not. She grinned again. Nothing like doing things in reverse.

As they pushed in their chairs to leave, one of the truckies called after them. 'Hey, girls, which one of you pretends to be the man?'

'You do,' she threw over her shoulder. The door slammed shut on his mates' roars of laughter.

The two old men came out to watch her back the station wagon up the driveway.

'You be careful of my gatepost, girlie!'

'Sure, sure.' She kissed Len, noticing the new lines on his face, and then shook Francis's hand. Letitia stood awkwardly behind her, like a dancer caught off balance mid-step. She moved to shake Len's hand but he caught her up and hugged her instead.

'You're early, darl. We weren't expecting you for another hour.'

'I drove like a fiend, just to see you, Len.'

The walls inside the house were still pale and smooth as eggshells. She noticed the white marble David in its customary place next to the television and also noticed that it no longer made her cringe. Overhead, the fans whirred softly against the heat.

'We'll leave you girls to get tidied up. Lunch'll be in about an hour,' Len said.

She ran the shower and stood under the jet of water while she watched the smoke from Letitia's cigarette make a thin, blue column in the direction of the ceiling.

'Didn't you see much of him when you were a kid?'

'What do you think? My family were at once end of the continent and he was at the other. He came down to visit once, when I was about five but he was by himself, of course. That must have been before he met Francis.'

'Didn't he get on with your father?'

She paused, balanced on one foot, working the towel back and forth until the blood rose to her skin.

'It wasn't that they disliked each other. They were just different, that's all.'

'Still seems weird, only seeing each other once in thirty years.'

'We're not all as tribal as you Calabrians.'

'There's advantages in being tribal.'

'Yes. Like having plates thrown at you.'

In the afternoon, habit tangled them together and she woke to find strands of fine, black hair lying across her face. She heard the distant heartbeat and imagined the cells, unseen citizens of another country, going about their business, like well-ordered clerks entering tall, city buildings.

The four of them ate dinner – fish and a platter piled with big, roughly chopped cubes of melon and paw-paw. The news was full of the Bjelke-Petersen trial and was followed by a current affairs segment about his political career and his contribution to Queensland life.

'Bastard,' muttered her uncle, next to her.

They sat out on the veranda and watched the great slabs of pink and gold give way to ebbing grey light. On her way inside, she passed the master bedroom, paused in front of the smooth-covered bed, vast as an undiscovered continent in its solitary pool of light.

She slept fitfully but woke to a sky blue as an unbroken promise. In the kitchen, Len and Francis clattered dishes and cleaned, moving with the measured stiffness of old, fit men. She picked up a tea towel but subsided into a chair when Len held up his hand.

'We thought we'd take a picnic to the beach, you know, just lie in the sun for a while.'

'Suits me.' She watched them as they skirted each other, deftly stacking plates and bowls into a ceramic pyramid.

They took cheese and lettuce and tomatoes from the fridge and began to prepare lunch.

Len sliced the new loaf; the pieces fell symmetrically, all the same thickness. 'Your dad and I used to do this all the time when we were young.'

'Did you?' She tried to imagine Jeff cutting sandwiches but her knowledge of him wouldn't translate the image. 'You must have had to lasso him first.'

Her uncle made a sound like water trickling out of a rusty pipe. 'Neither of us had much choice. Our sisters had both married by then. Jeff and I used to go sailing a lot, before he married Dorothy and I...' His voice trailed off.

'...came up here,' she finished for him.

They piled into the station wagon and followed the other cars moving in a tide toward the beach. She watched the kids, grinning as they waved or poked out their tongues, noses pressed against the glass of their parents' rear windows. Every milk bar they passed bore the same legend: 'Joh Jury Deciding'.

By the time they arrived, the beach was clogged with people. They found a place against the bluestone wall which demarcated sand from grass and she pushed the Esky belonging to the people sitting next door a few surreptitious inches away with her toe. Len opened a striped canvas deckchair and sat back, hat sliding over his eyes. She couldn't see his face any more, just limbs and a torso covered with grizzled hair.

'Come for a walk, Len.' Letitia was pulling a wide straw hat onto hair still wet from the shower.

'Not me, love, gotta look after this.' He patted his naked paunch complacently.

Lizard-like, she lay on the sand, and watched Francis and Letitia until their figures dwindled into black specks which she couldn't tell apart. She felt the heat seep through the thin towel, burning her legs. All around her were the sounds of families at play, mothers scolding children and children eating too much sweet, sticky food. Couples rubbed suntan oil over each other and adolescent boys chased shrieking girls into the water. She watched them all, trying to guess their secrets, the dark currents which flowed beneath the surface of their lives. She remembered the expression on Letitia's father's face the night he hurled the shard of crockery at her. Yes, she thought, he meant to kill me then. She tried to imagine the rage, the monumental pride, but the heavy sun drugged her and dragged her down, obliterating memory.

'Jesus!'

She woke to Len's muffled oath and watched, thick-eyed, as he clambered to his feet and began to run towards two figures crouched at the water's edge. His arms splayed out from his sides as he lumbered stubbornly on, like a boy in a schoolyard who persists in following a group of kids who don't want to play with him. He slowed to a stop in front of Francis, began to reach out for him but then suddenly jerked back, as though someone had tugged on the end of an invisible string. He stood there for a moment, just looking at the other man, and something passed between them, an acknowledgement of some ancient and unwritten rule. Awkward-jointed as a puppet, Len reached over and patted him on the shoulder. It was Letitia who helped Francis to his feet and who supported his weight as they both came slowly towards her over the sand. Len didn't move, just stood looking out at the pale, rippling water, face expressionless as he turned to follow.

'He slipped,' said Letitia, wadding up a towel and dabbing at blood oozing viscous as sap from the wound on Francis's knee. 'He needs…'

'I know what he needs, girlie,' said Len harshly, pushing in the tubular legs of the deckchair. 'Come on, let's get going. Plenty of stuff at home.'

They folded up the rest of the gear and made their way back to the house in silence.

On the way home, a news break announced that the ex-premier had been acquitted. She looked at her uncle's face and said nothing.

That night, wrapped around each other like two women drowning, they went down to the depths, came up holding each other, hair streaming dense as seaweed, eyes calm with knowledge and certainty.

In the morning, they spread the map over the breakfast table, added up the kilometres and wondered whether the car would make it. She tried to visualise the dots and disjointed lines as roads and railway tracks and towns inhabited by flesh and blood people. Absent-mindedly she traced the hair-fine line on her cheekbone and thought that the human body was a wonderful thing.

Outside, the heat was closing in and some of the carefully tended plants already drooped under the sun.

'Lovely to see you again, love,' said Len. 'Give my regards to Jeff and Dorothy.'

'Will do. You should come down sometime.'

'Yeah, well, maybe…' he said, looking over her shoulder at the front fence.

She kissed him, then Francis surprised her by putting his arms around her and giving her a hug.

'Be careful,' he said, and his long, fine hands flecked with age momentarily held her own. There was, suddenly, a look of utter longing on his face; she turned away and muttered something about how of course she would.

As she swung the car out of the driveway, she caught sight of them in the rear-view mirror, standing side by side in front of their neat white house.

'If I venture into the slipstream / by the viaduct of your dream,' sang Van Morrison from the tape deck. She sounded the horn once and the car turned into the street, heading north.

The Vixen

Two boys set out in a ute on a sunny summer afternoon. They had Lee Kernaghan on the tape deck, a six-pack of Bundy and Coke sitting between them on the seat and frangers in the glovebox. Brett had a cigarette in one hand and the other on the steering wheel. A trail of smoke drifted through the open window in the direction of the town behind them.

'Jeez, she's a real scorcher today.'

'Yeah, I reckon.' Denny helped himself to a smoke. He didn't like them, and his Uncle Terry, who had emphysema, was always pointing to the place where the top joint of his left hand little finger had been; but everyone Denny knew smoked. Chicks liked it if you smoked and there would be a shit-load of chicks where they were going tonight. A shit-load. He drew the smoke into his lungs and passed Brett a can.

'Ta, mate.' Brett tore the top off his can and flicked his cigarette butt out the window.

'Hey, be careful! You might start a fire!'

'You're an old woman.'

'And you're a ratbag.'

They had always carried on like this, Denny and Brett, ever since they had played in the sandpit in primary school, running their toy trucks and graders through the castles made by squealing girls. Girls! Denny glanced across at Brett, at the sun glinting off the wiry gold hairs on his forearms and at the tinder-yellow paddocks drenched with haze. The land around here was like nothing he had ever seen: down home, in the summer, it got dry, but the heat never gave you this bone-cracking, eye-watering feeling as you watched the road stretch in a ribbon between paddocks of razed wheat. Brett's old brother had been good: he'd paid them pretty well for helping with the harvest but that was all done now. They'd thrown their swags in the back of the ute and headed off this morning. They had been going to go straight home, drive all night taking turns at the wheel even though Denny hadn't got his licence yet, but when they stopped at the general store on the way out of town to get the Bundy and smokes, the woman at the counter had told them what they could do instead.

'Youse blokes on the way to the B&S ball?' and then she'd pulled out the local paper which Brett and Denny hadn't bothered reading while they were there because they'd been so flat out. The woman behind the counter seemed to think they should go. 'Youse might do yourself some good,' and she had winked and gone out the back to get the Bundy.

She was pretty old, about forty, but not too bad. She'd kept her figure, although the sun had given her a face you'd be able to crack rocks on in a couple of years. She'd winked at Brett again when he put the packet of frangers on top of the Bundy. 'Nice-lookin' boy like you shouldn't have any problems.' She hadn't taken any notice of Denny, standing behind Brett and watching him joking around, his blue eyes laughing down at her from underneath the dark blue cap.

'Hey, mate, I reckon she really fancied you,' Denny said, when they were back in the ute. 'I reckon you could have scored there.'

'Mate, she might have been all right with a paper bag over her head.' Brett eased the ute past a semi loaded with Aberdeen Angus; for a moment there was a heavy reek of shit then the air smelt like dust again. 'There'll be better-lookin' pieces where we're goin' tonight. The thing about older ladies,' and here he grinned knowingly, 'the thing about older ladies, mate, is that they're experienced. And they're often really randy.'

'You're full of bull.'

'No, mate. I know. True story.'

Brett touched the accelerator and the red ute, its rear window emblazoned with the RM Williams logo and telling the world it was a RUM PIG, shot forward.

Twenty minutes later, they reached the turn-off to home but instead of going west they headed in the opposite direction, away from the promise of green-shadowed creeks, towards the desert. Denny looked at his watch. He needed to piss. Up ahead, a tawny shape moved nonchalantly through a shorn paddock. Denny squinted and waited for it to take form. The tail gave the clue: the shape dissolved to a reddish ripple that faded into the heat and dust. There was another one a bit further along, then another and another.

'Gee, these foxes are thick on the ground.'

Brett grunted, his eyes not leaving the road. 'No one kills them around here. There's no sheep or calves to worry about, so they just run wild. That's why they're everywhere.'

They were everywhere, all along the rim of that sun-charred road, watching the ute as it passed. Denny saw one draped like a feral ornament along the straggling branches of a solitary gum; its eyes gleamed bright as fire. He started counting. Foxes mainly came out at night but here they seemed to be fierce daylight predators. There was one old dog-fox with three legs – it must have been caught in a trap – and another with something grey clutched between its jaws.

Brett leaned across to change the tape; their wrists brushed and a number jumped out of Denny's mouth.

'Ten! Ten foxes, just in the last fifty ks!'

'Yeah, good, mate.'

Gina Jefferies's pretty blonde voice told them both that she was missing her man and Brett turned the sound up.

'I need to splash the boots, mate. This Bundy has gone straight through me.' He stopped the ute near a small bridge and strolled in the direction of a big tree overhanging barbed wire and throwing its shade almost to the road.

A storm water culvert ran beneath the bridge. When it rained here, it would come straight down, the water pushing everything before it. Denny unzipped then grunted with relief as he let everything out. He glanced over to where Brett stood straddled and spraying. He was taller and broader than Denny. The sun had soaked his T-shirt and sweat ran in a dark ridge between his shoulder blades. He finished, shook himself and turned. Denny looked away. The air smelt of eucalyptus and piss and dry earth. He looked at Brett's arms, at the gold hair laid over the swell of muscle. Denny felt like a sook, like a girl; he didn't know why Brett still hung around with him. On the other side of the barbed wire he saw a plumed tail, sharp ears and a snout. Denny looked at it. He looked at Brett,

'You know, I reckon I could catch one of those foxes.'

'Bullshit.'

'No, I reckon I could.'

'I bet ya can't.'

'Can so.' Denny slid carefully under the fence.

The fox stopped with one paw raised in mid-air and regarded him enquiringly. 'Catch me if you can,' she seemed to say and Denny thought she looked at him in a teasing sort of way; inviting. He followed her down the bank of the creek bed and under the bridge.

There was a dense musty smell of fox and her shadow cast a bluish sliding blur along the culvert. Denny squatted down. Heat from the culvert spiked his temples and for a moment he thought he'd pass out but in the end she came easily into his arms. He felt the sharp beat of her heart behind the small pointed breast bone, the rasp of her breath and the long coarse hairs of her tail against his naked arms.

'That bloody thing'll get fleas everywhere,' Brett complained when Denny carried her to the car.

'She'll be right.' He settled the fox on his lap, his arms loosely encircling her and she seemed happy enough, sticking her snout out of the open window.

'How do you know it's a "she"?'

'I'm sure it's a little girl.'

'Yeah, but how can you tell?'

'By the way she looked at me.' Denny knew this sounded stupid. He went on quickly. 'What's a female fox called?'

'A vixen.'

Vixen. Now Denny remembered. He remembered that a pretty girl was called a fox. Didn't Uncle Terry, that old bugger with his beer face and whisky nose, have a vinyl record by some guy from the sixties? Some black guy who died… Oh, foxy lady…Denny closed his eyes and opened then to Brett's grin.

'You look like a right drop kick.'

'I was just thinkin', thinking' about home. D'ya want me to drive for a while?'

'No, mate, you look pretty comfy with your girlfriend.'

'I think I'll keep her, build a little run for her in the backyard. She'll get on all right with Hercules. Dogs and foxes can be taught to get on all right together, can't they?'

'You're a poofta, mate,' Brett said affectionately, crushing the last empty can of Bundy and dropping it onto the floor.

Long weals of pink light flamed then died and explosions of gold-edged cloud knotted the sky and disappeared. All the empty paddocks greyed and faded to darkness. At home, Uncle Terry would be taking the top off the third bottle. Denny's mum would be sitting on the sofa reading. She would have fried Uncle Denny his chops or steak in butter, the way he liked things cooked, before making something for herself. Afterwards she would have settled down to read, ignoring the television and Uncle Terry's occasional ramblings. They hardly ever talked, even though they spent most of their time together; that is, when Uncle Terry wasn't in the pub.

'I've come to look after youse,' he'd announced, plopping his suitcase on the front doorstep, six months after the grader had rolled over Denny's dad on that embankment just out of town.

It had given Denny's mum something to do, cooking and cleaning for her brother-in-law. She had been in a bad way for a while but then, there were people who thought Denny's mum was a bit funny, anyway. Going to the library was all right: lots of ladies did that. But buying all those books at op shops, that was going a bit far.

The books sat around in great mouldering piles, 'growing dust', as

Uncle Terry said, when he walked past them and gave one of the piles a kick. 'Bloody books,' he'd growl.

He was a funny old bugger, was Uncle Terry. Only the other night he'd interrupted Denny's mum when she had been reading *The Women's Room* and really gone to town. 'You women think you've done it really hard. Well, let me tell you something! Us blokes are going to run into the street and burn our blue singlets. Tear off our blue singlets and burn them! You women want romance, well, you've got to earn it! Get down on your knees and earn it!'

Denny's mum had just looked at him, waited until he finished and gone back to her reading but later Denny had asked him what he meant about the blue singlets.

Uncle Terry had winked and grinned. 'You know how women burned their bras to get equal rights? Well, we blokes are going to burn our blue singlets.' Yeah, he was a funny old bugger, was Uncle Terry.

Something bit Denny – bit him hard. He looked down. A brown track moved along his arms. Shit. Fleas! The vixen moved restlessly. She sniffed the air and let out a low whine.

'Pull over, mate. I'm gunna let her out for a minute. I think she needs to piss.'

There was an old piece of baling twine coiled limp as a dead snake on the floor of the ute and Denny fixed it around the vixen's neck. 'Come on, girl.'

She squatted down like a little red dog to do her business then whined again and lashed her tail but she didn't resist when he gathered her up determinedly.

'What are you gunna do with her when we get there?' Brett reached for his lighter and lit a cigarette.

'I dunno. Maybe we could just tie her up.'

'She'll chew through the rope.'

'We could leave her in the ute.'

'I'm not having that thing dropping fleas and pissing all over the seats.'

'We could just tie her up,' repeated Denny stubbornly. 'She mightn't run away.'

Brett looked at him as though he was mental. His eyes went back to the road now crowded with a crawling procession of utes and cars. The vixen stirred in Denny's arms and snuffed the air as they turned off the road and down a dusty intermittent track, its outlines smudged to powder beneath the headlights. DRINK TILL HE'S EYE CANDY: a metallic blue ute cut in front of them and Brett hit the horn.

'Look at that fat chick,' he said disgustedly, as the chunky blonde driving gave a cheery wave. 'There oughtta be a law against chicks like that!' He leaned on the horn again and gunned the engine.

The blonde gave another wave.

They followed her all the way down the track to the gaunt twin cypresses flanking the gate of the recreation reserve. Denny saw the floodlit oval with its makeshift stage and the low clubhouse behind it. More cypresses, windblown and emaciated, fenced one side of the rec reserve; some of their dead grey branches had been chain-sawed off then heaped together. Against a black sky littered with stars, the bonfire burned with a crackly oily sound and spat up handfuls of sparks. Brett gave the bloke on the gate money; it was a lot of money but it meant you could drink as much as you liked, all night.

The bloke gave them the hairy eyeball. 'You fellas had better put ya ties on.'

'What ties?'

'Ya black ties. Are youse from Melbourne? Doncha know ya always wear a black tie to a B&S?'

Denny broke out in a sweat. He felt like an idiot. He didn't dare look at Brett. He was scared shitless about tonight, but, jeez, he wanted to be here. To have come all this way for nothing...

The bloke gave an exasperated sigh, reached into his pocket and pulled out two black cloth strings. 'I always keep a few handy, just for dickheads like you.' He handed over the ties.

'Thanks, mate!' Brett chucked one across to Denny. It was crumpled and stained with something white. 'We'll give them back at the end of the night.'

The bloke grunted. 'By the end of the night, you'll be lucky to know your own name. Now, piss off.' He waved them in.

'Shit, that was close.'

'I reckon.' Denny hugged the vixen closer. He felt like a real fuckhead. Melbourne. Christ, what an insult. Brett parked the ute then knotted his tie over his T-shirt.

'I'll go and get some grog. You work out what to do with her.' He gestured towards the vixen then disappeared in the direction of the clubhouse. Denny sat in the car for a while, just looking around. More and more blokes and chicks were arriving, the chicks in long formal dresses, the blokes in any old thing but they all wore a black tie. A bloke went past who looked a lot like Brett, tall and blonde but with broader shoulders. He wore jeans with a ruffled white shirt and a suit jacket over it, a get-up which would have made Denny look like a dag but on this guy it was grouse, really cool.

Denny cuddled the vixen, still thinking. Suddenly, he knew what to do. He nestled the vixen under one arm and manoeuvred them both out of the ute. He took the rope, tied it around her then tied the other end around a rear tyre. He took out the tarp lying in the ute tray and started tying it on. It was a bit hard, the vixen kept making little darts and starts but he got it on, left one corner free, then tied her in. She should have water. Denny looked around.

'Oh, look, what have you got there?' exclaimed a voice behind him, and when Denny turned around he saw the chunky blonde chick, wearing a strapless pale blue dress with a full skirt. She bulged a bit over the top and a pair of sturdy Blundstone boots poked out beneath the skirt.

There was another girl with her, dark-haired and wearing red. She was really pretty, Denny saw, with a catch in his throat, like a girl out of a magazine.

'Oh, look!' cried the blonde girl. 'Oh, she's cute! Can we pat her?'

'She's got fleas,' said Denny nervously. He wanted to make a good impression, didn't want the girls to get bitten or to get their dresses dirty but they managed all right, petting the vixen and cooing out 'darling' and 'sweetie'.

'She can't stay here,' said the blonde. 'It's too hot for her.'

'I know,' said Denny wretchedly, 'but I dunno what else to do.'

'I do,' said the blonde and she shot off to her ute.

Denny stood around awkwardly, trying to think of something to say to her friend. 'Fair turnout,' he muttered but she ignored him, then the blonde girl was back with a wooden crate.

'Been helping a mate move house,' she explained.

The crate became a hutch underneath one of the big cypresses. They found a discarded ice cream container and a tap.

'There you go,' said the blonde. 'Now she's got her own little beer garden.' She turned and held out her hand. 'Zoe.' She indicated the brunette. 'Larissa.'

'Denny.' Denny shifted from one foot to another.

Just then, Brett came back carrying the cans. 'Gidday, girls. Here, dickhead, catch.'

He threw the beer to Denny, who let the cold metal, devious as a fish, slip through his fingers. The girls laughed.

'Don't mind him,' said Brett. 'He comes from a real backward place. His parents were related.'

They laughed again.

Brett put his arm around Denny's shoulders and hugged him so hard he was pulled off balance. 'Come on, let's get going.'

The first band was already playing and they started towards the stage, with Brett and Larissa leading. Denny couldn't hear what Brett said but he saw Larissa reach up and tug at the peak of his cap, the one with the John Deere logo, while her pretty pointed face laughed up from beneath the black Akubra she wore. Her long red dress was made from some shiny sort of material which gleamed and twisted like fire.

Denny knew what Uncle Terry would say about Larissa: 'Go after her! She's got nice tits and a nice tight little arse. Go after her! Don't worry about the fat girl!'

Denny glanced across at Zoe but her eyes were on Brett as he stopped to light cigarettes for himself and Larissa. She'd rather be walking with him. Denny didn't blame her. Nevertheless, he thought he'd better make conversation. 'Fair turnout,' he said, swigging from his can.

'Yeah, not bad,' Zoe agreed. 'You been here before?'

'Nah, this is my first.' As soon as the words were out of Denny's mouth, he realised how piss-weak they made him sound.

'Your first B&S? You're shitting me!' Zoe tilted the half bottle of Bundy she held then drank; a small sticky trickle ran down her chin. 'Hey, you guys,' she called to Brett and Larissa, 'this bloke's a B&S virgin!'

Brett turned around, grinning. 'Maybe you could break him in.'

Denny was glad it was dark because they couldn't see him going red while they laughed. He hated that he was seventeen and had never been with anyone – although, of course, when the guys talked about it, he always made out he'd been with plenty of chicks. But Brett knew; Brett knew everything about him.

'Well, Mr B&S Virgin, we're going to have to show you a really good time!' Zoe held out the bottle of Bundy.

'Ta.' Denny watched as she poured it into his can.

'My plez.' Zoe had chubby hands hardened with small yellow calluses. When he asked her what her job was, she winked.

'Horsebreaker.'

'Bull…' Denny felt himself redden again.

'No bull, I'm in partnership with Dad. We do breaking, training, whatever. What about yourself?'

'Motor mechanic. Apprentice.'

'Oh, babe,' she punched his arm lightly. 'You could tune my engine any day.'

Denny laughed. He could tell she wasn't really interested in him but he liked her anyway. He felt comfortable with her, the way you might feel if you were talking to a sister, not that he had ever had one of those. His own sister had died when she was two and Denny was just a baby. Meningitis: that was what had killed his sister. 'Your mother was never the same, never the same after that,' Uncle Terry told him one evening, halfway through the third bottle. 'It just about killed the poor hooer.' Denny's mother never talked about it.

Families could be sad things, Denny knew that, but Zoe's didn't sound that bad. She talked about her dad, the horsebreaker and ex-rodeo rider, 'a really ace bloke', her mum, 'who just stays at home being a mum, but she's great', her brother at ag college, her other brother at secondary school and her little sister, 'who's not like me at all, she has ballet lessons and stuff. She likes to, you know…' Here, Zoe demonstrated a tipsy pirouette. One boot caught the hem of the pale blue dress and, as the four of them reached the stage, she came crashing down.

'Oh, jeez, pissed again!' she exclaimed cheerfully.

Denny was getting pretty pissed himself because all along the way Zoe had been topping up his cans with the Bundy. He felt a bit sick, actually, but he wasn't going to let on to anyone, especially Brett, although it was unlikely Brett would notice. He had his arm around Larissa, holding her close.

'Dance?' screamed Zoe and she took his hand and they forged through the crowd.

Denny caught the caramel smell of the rum on her breath and saw the neat semicircles which darkened the bodice of her dress under the arms. People bumped and jostled; he lost sight of Larissa and Brett. He tried to move in time to the music, heard the wail of a slide guitar as the singer told him about a dark wreath of roses on a grave. That was sad, Denny thought, closing his eyes and giving himself over. It was sad that the guy had lost the girl he loved but maybe he'd find someone else one day. What was it Uncle Terry said? 'There's more than one pebble on the beach, more than one fish in the sea.'

Denny laughed out loud.

Someone elbowed him in the ribs and he thought it was Zoe telling him not to be a dickhead but it was just some bloke trying to get to the bar. ''Scuse, me, mate.' He towed a small redhead wearing a lot of slutty black eye make-up and a black dress.

Denny looked around; he couldn't see Zoe anywhere. She'd vanished, just like the girl in the song. Shit.

The beer lurched sourly in his belly underneath its oily coating of rum. He needed to piss. He kept bumping into people as he fought his way through the dancers. 'Sorry…sorry…' he muttered, battering his way towards what he hoped was the edge of the crowd

'Hey, no worries, mate!' A bloke clapped him jovially on the back. 'Hey, stay and party, mate!'

'I gotta find my friends,' muttered Denny. 'I gotta go.'

'Well, when you've gotta go, you've gotta go, mate!' The bloke clapped him on the back again. 'Hey, mate, suck more piss!' He raised his stubby in a departing salute.

'Yeah, good, mate.' Denny raised his can then, realising it was empty, threw it on the ground. He needed to piss so bad it hurt.

He looked around for a handy tree then noticed a bloke just hanging it out in the open. Denny didn't think that was right and was heading for one of the cypresses when he saw, he nearly tripped over her, a girl squatting on the ground, her dress fanned out like a tent. Now, that was disgusting. Blokes might do that sort of thing but not chicks. He saw another girl doing the same, now that was REALLY DISGUSTING. It was like something an animal would do.

Denny reached the cypresses and sprayed the scaly grey bark. As he zipped up, he almost stepped in a puddle of vomit at the foot of the tree. There were a couple of other blokes emptying their guts no far away and the smell made Denny's stomach shudder and clench all over again.

'I gotta get outta here, I gotta find Brett,' but Brett wouldn't want to be bothered with him, he never did want to be bothered with Denny once the night got going.

He should try to find the vixen and make sure she was all right. She would be scared, away from everything she knew and wondering what all the noise was about. Denny hoped no one had interfered with her or started teasing her, because drinking turned some people into animals. He didn't want her to get hurt.

He stumbled in the direction of the bonfire, staggering around couples locked together or sprawled on the ground. Everyone seemed to have found someone to have a good time with; he must be some kind of freak, to have only a fox to talk to.

The bonfire's flames leapt and twisted while he tried to remember where the vixen was. 'C'mon, baby, light my fire…' Denny started laughing and staggering around. The song was another old favourite of Uncle Terry's but he couldn't remember what came next. 'Light my fire…light my fire…' There was music coming from somewhere, he could hear it.

Denny shook his head from side to side. He looked around. The music disappeared, gusted out at him again. Ahhh. It was coming through the lighted window of the white caravan behind him. Denny tottered up the steps and opened the door. For a second, the light blinded him then he saw Elvis sitting in front of a mirror.

'Well, hello there, son.'

'Oh, it's you!' exclaimed Denny. 'What are you doing here?'

'All the world's a stage, boy, upon which man is born to strut and fret his hour,' Elvis replied.

Then Denny got it. Jeez, he must be more pissed than he thought.

'You're not him! You're not real!'

'Excuse me?' Elvis smoothed the top of his glowing black pompadour. 'I'm the boss act tonight, boy.' He went back to turning the dial on the old transistor radio in front of him. Blasts of static alternated with Shania Twain. 'Country, country,' muttered Elvis. 'Nothing but fuckin' country.'

'We're in the country,' Denny said, helpfully.

'Oh, I know that, boy.' Abruptly, the southern accent fell away and

Elvis started to sound just like an ordinary bloke. 'Believe you me, I know that. You don't come all the way from Parra-bloody-matta and not know you're in the country.'

He turned back to the mirror, underneath which, on a low table, lay a clutter of brushes, bottles and tubes. There was also a fifth of Johnny Walker and a couple of shot glasses. A big spangly yellow crucifix dangled above the mirror.

'Drink?' asked Elvis, reaching for the bottle.

'Ta.' Then because Denny knew he was being a bit rude staring at the guy, he held out his hand. 'Denny Serle.'

'Johnny O'Hallaran.' He poured out the Scotch and handed it to Denny. Up close, he wasn't really like the King at all. He had the hair and the black leather pants and but that was it. He was skinny, not big and fat like the King got; he didn't have the King's big sidies. He didn't even have a chin. He was dark-skinned and looked like some kind of wog.

Denny glanced around. There was a double bed down one end of the caravan covered with a shiny blue spread and a couple of big cushions fluffed up on it. There was a built-in wardrobe with a glittery white catsuit hanging off the doorknob. The guy must change costumes during the show. There was a big framed photo on the wall: Johnny, a woman, two boys and a girl.

'That's my missus and kiddies.'

'Nice,' said Denny. 'Real nice.'

'Oh, yeah,' said Johnny O'Hallaran. 'Light of my life. Kids all grown-up now, of course.' He held up the bottle again. 'Chin, chin?'

'Ta.' Denny didn't throw this one straight down. He took a sip and watched Johnny pick up a fat brush and start dusting his face with powder.

Powder! 'You put on make-up?' Denny asked nervously.

'Sure.' Johnny didn't take his eyes from the mirror. He reached for a thick black pencil and started outlining his eyes. 'You don't put this stuff on, the audience can't see your face at all. You're just a little pink blob to them, boy.' He dropped into the Elvis voice. 'Yes, sir, just a little pink blob.'

He was touching his cheeks with some kind of red stuff Denny had once seen a chick put on at school. It was weird but kind of interesting, too. Denny's mother never wore make-up, not even lipstick to go out, not that she went out much, only to shop and buy the books. And what would Uncle Terry say? That the bloke was some kind of poofta, for sure. But it was kind of cool, too. Johnny looked totally different now.

'What songs do you do?' Denny leaned forward.

'All the old standards.' Johnny opened a small box, fished out something hairy. '"Hound Dog", "Jailhouse Rock", "Heartbreak Hotel". The second half, when it's getting late and people want to get up close and personal I do the ballads: "In the Ghetto", "Can't Help Falling in Love", "Cold Kentucky Rain".'

Johnny O'Hallaran smoothed the sideburns down firmly. 'I've never been able to grow much,' he muttered under his breath. 'Yes, sir, people do like a good ballad, indeed they do.'

'Have you always done this? You know, been Elvis?'

'I used to do the rissole circuit, up north.'

'Rissole?' said Denny, helping himself to the Scotch.

'The RSL, the rissole,' explained Johnny O'Hallaran patiently. 'In New South and Queensland. I was big up there for a while. I used to do Judy, Barbara, Dusty…'

'Women?'

'I only want to be with you…' Johnny O'Hallaran trilled suddenly and Denny nearly fell off his chair. He had no idea a bloke could sound like that! Johnny flipped open the suitcase at his feet. He took out a curly platinum blonde wig. There were others, Denny saw, all different colours and styles. 'Here, put this on.'

'Piss off!' Denny shrank back.

'No, here, put it on.' Johnny O'Hallaran shook it at him, the way you would shake a dog that had shat inside. 'Go on, just for a rage.'

Denny put down his drink. He let Johnny pull the wig down and watched him in the mirror tucking in a few stray wisps of dark hair.

'Oh, doesn't she look beau-ti-ful,' murmured Johnny O'Hallaran. He went over to the cupboard and took out a gold-sequinned, black chiffon dress which he held against Denny.

'I'm not putting that on! No fuckin' way!'

'There, there, dear, settle down.' Johnny put the dress back in the cupboard. He picked up a dark pink crayon and outlined his lips, then coloured them so that they looked rubbery and full as sausages.

'Do ya do ya own hair?' Denny blurted.

'I do now,' Johnny replied. 'Never used to, once, but it's got too much grey in it now. That's not much trouble. The hair's the easy part.'

Yeah, the hair was the easy part, as long as you had some. The hair was the least of your worries when you had Hester the Molester on your arse telling you that you had to 'upgrade your act' and talking about the website for Registered Tribute Artists. 'They're all younger than you,' as though it was a fucking crime. Everyone was fucking younger than he was now. Shit, some of the parents of these kids here tonight weren't born when he was Johnny O leading his neat little combo the Half Tones and playing the pubs and clubs around Charleston and Bundaberg and all up and down the coast.

That's where he met Hester, back in 1967, in a break between sets at the Trocadero Club in Kempsey. Even back then, dressed in his blue polyester suit and carrying a briefcase, it had been pretty obvious what he was, the little fairy, trying to take the quickstep out of his walk on the way back to the bar, telling him rock 'n' roll was finished: 'Everyone knows that except these rednecks around here. You've got to move with the times.'

So then it was long hair, paisley shirts and multicoloured strobes: Hester turned us into John & Dave's Plastic Adventure. That didn't last but by the time it was over the poofta movement had started up, there were all kinds of bars and clubs wanting to hear Judy and Barbara and Dusty. All through the seventies I did the girls, right into the eighties until the disease started killing off the pooftas and making the ones left stay home at night. So then it was the rissole circuit, couples wanting a night out or groups of older people wanting the same 'but nothing too blue on account of the women folk.' Adapt and change, adapt and change, that's what it's always been about. People like this young whipper-snapper didn't understand that, they didn't have a fucking clue.

Johnny gave his face the final once over with powder. 'Have you seen *Priscilla, Queen of the Desert?*'

'Oh, yeah, I seen that movie,' said Denny. He and Brett had seen it when it came to town and laughed themselves silly.

'I used to do Priscilla at parties. That was huge for me, for a while.' Johnny faced the crucifix and crossed himself. 'Show time. What's the crowd like tonight, boy?' he asked in the Elvis voice.

'Good. Real good.'

'Well, that's good.' Johnny refilled their glasses. He took a playful swipe at Denny with the brush and, when he didn't resist, dusted his nose and cheeks.

Denny downed the Scotch. He closed his eyes and gave himself up to the whisper and tickle of the brush. He let Johnny outline his eyes with thick black pencil then coat his eyelids with blue. Johnny streaked Denny's cheeks with crumbly pink.

'I just can't help believing as she slips her hand in mine and my fingers close around it like a glove…' he sang under his breath. He rose and held out his hand. 'Dance?'

'Oh, get fucked…'

'Oh, come on, don't be such a drag,' said Johnny and Denny laughed. He had to, it was so fucking funny. Johnny held him in his arms and they started to waltz. It was a bit of a squeeze in the caravan. They crashed into a couple of chairs and Denny almost lost his balance. 'Oopsy, pet, have a care.'

As Johnny hauled him up, Denny caught sight of himself in the mirror: the round pink spots of rouge and the big red mouth underneath the bright yellow ringlets. He didn't look like a girl. He looked like a fucking clown! He pulled the wig off and blundered to the caravan door, trailed by Johnny O'Hallaran's hyena laugh.

Denny flung the wig away and it landed then settled like a small furry animal beneath one of the cypress trees. Denny laughed. He staggered then spewed. He spewed his fucking guts up then wiped his mouth with the back of his hand. He felt sick. He wanted to lie down in the ute with the vixen and sleep for a month. He stopped for a piss and stood still, trying to figure out where things were. There was the fire…there was the stage…the ute must be…

Denny staggered away from the flames, towards the row of cypress. The moon had risen while he had been in the caravan and he could just make out two figures moving rhythmically. The woman was on all fours, her pale blue dress rolled down to her waist, large white tits dangling, being fucked like a farm animal as she grunted and moaned, eyes rolled back in her head. The face of the thrusting man was obscured by the cap he hadn't bothered to remove, the cap with the John Deere logo.

Denny bent over again but there was nothing left except strings of yellow bile. He stumbled on.

The vixen still crouched in her makeshift pen. Denny dropped to his knees and peered in. She snarled. There was a bloody ring at the top of her paw where her teeth had peeled back the fur. Denny saw the white glisten of bone. He stared into her amber eyes and saw hatred, also shame, as though she thought she was mutilated and defective.

Denny grasped the crate and lifted it away. The vixen saw freedom but didn't move.

'Well, go on,' said Denny. 'What are you waiting for?'

Still the vixen crouched, motionless, then suddenly she shot forward, her coat a tawny spurt. Denny was hoping she would stop, just once, and look back but in a second she was a fire-tailed smudge and then she was out of sight.

Denny stayed where he was, kneeling and bent over, forearms

braced along the length of his thighs. He was glad that he had let her go but he was worried too.

She was a wild thing that needed to be free but she was out there on her own, cut off from everything she knew. Would she survive in this strange new place? Wouldn't she always be looking for a way back to the life she had come from, even though she might make a new lair and find other foxes?

The make-up which he hadn't rubbed off glistened in the moonlight, as he tried to think things out but the effort was too much. He rolled onto his side next to the ute and closed his eyes. There was no one to help him with the answers to any questions, for, like the vixen, he was a long way from home.

Little Miss Tiny Tots

All down the highway, Audrey kept wanting to change her dress. She just wouldn't shut up. He sat behind the wheel trying to blank her voice as the grey kilometres scrolled by but in the end he gave in.

'Yeah, all right, we'll stop soon and you can have a look for it.'

The pink travelling case containing her clothes and cosmetics had been packed in a flurry; her shoes had been thrown in on top of everything and then the zip jammed. He hoped she wouldn't find something missing and start making a scene. He would have liked to have gone a bit further, to have put some more distance between them and the lines of familiar houses but he knew what she was like when she got going and, anyway, the sun had come out and pretty soon they'd start to bake in this shit-box that didn't have proper air-con.

'When are we going to stop? I want to pee!'

'Yeah, we'll stop soon, sweetheart, just over the top of this next hill.'

He remembered this town, remembered coming here years ago to see his mate Baz, who'd just set up a panel beating business. He remembered the trees big as houses down the grassy avenue dividing the main street, him and Baz hanging wheelies underneath the clock tower after midnight with two giggling chicks they'd picked up at the Continental Hotel. One had pissed off home but later he and Baz had gone through her friend on the back seat. Young blokes' stuff. Now he had the sun belting thought the windscreen and Audrey jabbering in his ear and it was with relief that he crested the hill and saw the squat brown toilet block ahead. He pulled over, got out and opened the door.

'You wait for me, princess,' but she was already running ahead, so he had no choice but to follow her into the entrance marked 'Ladies'.

He fumbled in the pink case for the braid-trimmed dress then bent down to help Audrey pull it on but his fingers stumbled over the unfamiliar fastenings.

'I can do it!' She turned irritably away and closed the small pearl buttons herself.

She hadn't had enough sleep; neither had he. All week, lying awake in the dingy flat, his scheme had festered like an open sore: if he could just distract Helen for long enough and if Big Connie wasn't there... He'd dragged himself through work and been told off twice by the manager. It didn't matter, though, because in the end everything had gone according to plan.

'We're going on an adventure, princess,' he told her when they finally got away and she had seemed pleased enough, drumming her heels excitedly against the car seat as they drove through the petrochem plants and out through the western suburbs. Now, standing in the graffiti-splattered toilet, in front of a perspex mirror which gave back their streaky and imperfect images, she didn't seem so sure.

'I want plaits, Dad! And I'm hungry!'

'You only had breakfast a few minutes ago,' he joked.

'I want McDonalds!'

'I don't think there's McDonalds here, sweetheart. How about fish and chips?'

He couldn't manage the plaits. The blonde hair kept slipping though his fingers. In the end, he gave up and just brushed it out until it lay like a glimmery sheen on her shoulders. He didn't know where it came from: no one in his family had snowy hair like that and when Helen had named her after the famous movie star they had both expected a little brunette stunner.

'You're beautiful, baby. You're my girl.'

As they drove further into the town, he tried to remember where Baz's business had been but it was ten years ago, more... Here and there, vacant shopfronts gaped emptily but there were cars everywhere and the streets seemed clogged with people. He had to wait a while in the fish and chips shop but when he finally placed his order he asked the guy behind the counter about Baz.

'No, mate, never heard of him.' He turned back to his fryer, a big bloke running to fat, with time-blurred tattoos on both arms. 'Judy: True Love Never Dies' was wrapped around a naked woman and a flaming heart.

Oh, yeah. He could tell the fish and chip guy a few things about that-but probably nothing he didn't already know. Still, this imagined sense of kinship made for conversation.

'Seem to be a few people around today, mate.'

The guy grunted and heaved the glistening mound of chips onto paper. 'It's the show.'

'The show?'

'The agricultural show.'

'Oh, right.' Rednecks standing around looking at cows. Fat old women judging scones. 'Is there anything for little girls?'

'Whaddya mean?' The guy gave him a strange look.

'You know, a parade…' He floundered around, looking for the right word. 'A beauty contest…it's for my daughter.'

'Yeah, I think there's something like that.' The guy gave an indifferent shrug and drained the two pieces of flake. 'There's something like that.' He turned the fish onto the chips and poured a shower of salt over everything. 'How old's your kid?'

'Just four. That's her there.' As he put money for the food on the counter, he showed the photo in his wallet.

'Oh, yeah. She's gunna be a real little heart-breaker in a few years.'

'She already is!' Impossible to tell the guy about the overflowing billow of love around his heart the first time he held her. He hadn't minded getting up at 3 a.m. when she cried. The first little tutu she had owned for her contests, when she was just a little tacker and could barely stand up, he had it in a box in the flat somewhere.

He hurried out to the car, carrying the paper-wrapped parcel. 'I think I've got something for you, princess.'

The guy in the shop had given directions and pretty soon he saw the red and yellow seats of the ferris wheel, hanging in the air like stranded boats. There was a merry-go-round with about ten horses and a single row of sideshow clowns turned painted eyes first one way, then the other. Showjumpers stood in the centre of the arena, monumental haunches gleaming above steaming piles of shit. Through the open door of a corrugated-iron shed he glimpsed tiered cakes, pavilioned and curlicued with icing.

'Come on, baby.' There it was, a rickety wooden platform and a wooden shack with seats, behind it.

A hand-painted sign read, 'Little Miss Tiny Tots', except some wag had tried scratching out the 'o' and replacing it with an 'i'.

'Is it too late, too late to enter?'

'No, you're right,' smiled the big woman with JUDGE pinned to her chest. 'There's plenty of room for the little girl to change over there.' She pointed to another toilet block but he'd had enough of that for one day.

Hurriedly, he unpacked the travelling case from the car. It had taken only a moment, in Audrey's room, to fold up the white tutu with its spangled fairy wings, to stuff in the satin slippers and the spangled headband and then to sneak the whole lot out to the car. Stuff Helen, the maggot-eaten, power-hungry bitch, always going on about her rights. No one ever gave a shit about his rights. He'd turn a day into a long weekend: he and Audrey would have a ball! The tutu was a bit crushed but he managed to fluff it out. He did his best with her hair although any other time Helen would have done it up in big ice cream curls. He smoothed on a little bit of pink lipstick and touched the mascara wand to her lashes.

'You go and clean them up, sweetheart.' He gave her a little push and stood up to survey the competition as she trotted off.

There were half a dozen others, mainly done up in dresses, although one dark-skinned, dark-eyed, woggy-looking kid wore some kind of body stocking brightly patterned in red, green and yellow. All the girls wore make-up although one of the mothers had overdone it and plastered a freckle-faced moppet with glitter and blue pools of grease. He felt uncomfortable looking at her, a five-year-old with a whore's mouth and come-fuck-me eyes.

'All get in a line, please, girls!' The judge made them all stand facing her, looking from the makeshift stage.

Audrey was on one end of the line, face flushed and one hand kneading the stiff folds of tulle.

'Smile, princess,' he called, which drew a dark look from the old bitch.

'Now please walk around for me, girls.'

Audrey put her hands up in the air and did a little twirly turn, like a ballerina. The judge smiled and wrote something down on the notepad in her hand.

The contests had been Helen's idea. She had entered Audrey in one at the local shopping mall. By the end of the year, there had been a whole shelf of cups and trophies; by the time Audrey was three, they had had to buy a special cabinet to hold them.

'Sugar and spice and all things nice,' Helen used to chant, as she helped Audrey pull on the white tutu or the pink tutu or the mauve tutu and brushed the shining hair. 'Oh, Aud-drey…'

He'd back the four-wheel drive out of the garage and sound the horn. They'd walk down the path towards him, Helen wearing a dress or dark suit, not jeans and trainers like most of the other mums. She'd lead Audrey by the hand, shepherding her to the car and fastening the seat belt of the front passenger seat securely around her.

'And where would Miss Audrey like to go?' he'd ask, trying to sound like a Pommy chauffeur from an old movie and making her giggle and Helen laugh. They'd been a team, the whole three of them, Until Helen started bringing Big Connie's advice home form work.

'Connie thinks I have low self-esteem… Connie and I are going to a personal growth seminar this weekend…'

Personal growth! Wankers making money. They'd led Helen so far up the garden path it had turned into a one-way street. 'I need some time by myself.'

'Well, if you need so much time by yourself, I'll take Audrey.' But it turned out this wasn't what was meant. Helen should have been here; she would have taken charge and charmed the judge who was draping the blue sash over the woggy-looking kid in the body stocking. Second went to a redhead in a long ice-green gown, elbow-length gloves and diamante earrings. Audrey got third. He saw her blink up at the sun and clench her lower lip in her teeth as all the contestants made a final circuit of the stage. The woggy-looking kid did a big cartwheel and everybody laughed and clapped.

'We were looking for something just a *little* bit different this year,' he heard the big judge say to the woman who looked like the mother of that kid.

Cunts. He didn't care about their stupid little show. He'd just get his daughter and piss off. She came towards him, her cheeks splotched with red paint which matched the stain of heat rash bubbling on one leg.

He held out his arms. 'Third's not so bad, baby,' he said consolingly, stroking the shiny white sash.

'No good!' She struggled out of the satin coil and threw it on the ground. 'No good!' The ballerina slippers, scuffed and dirty, left grassy smudges on the sash. 'I wanta go home! I hate it here! Where's Mum? I wanta go home!'

'Yeah, okay, let's get outta here.' He'd seen one of the mothers raise her eyebrows at another.

The wind had come up; it was going to be a grey squally night. As they crossed the grass to the car, he remembered the business card, dog-eared, grease-stained at the back of his wallet. Worth a try.

'Hi, is Baz there?' he asked, when he rang the number on his mobile.

'Who's this?' asked a young male voice.

'Just tell him Bryon rang.' He suddenly felt really tired.

Audrey ran ahead, her tantrum forgotten, trying to do a cartwheel and giggling when she fell in a heap.

'You want to play, baby? You want to go on the swings?'

'Change, Dad.' She held up her arms. 'I'm cold.'

He helped her pull on the striped leggings and dark jumper that she chose. He managed to clumsily twist her hair into a flowered band to make a ponytail.

'Now we go home, Dad?'

'Not yet, kitten. We're going to take Uncle VisaCard and find a nice place to stay and watch telly and have all kinds of nice things to eat.'

'DVDs, Dad?'

'Yeah, DVDs.'

By the time they went to the only DVD place in town, chose *Harry Potter*, found out where the caravan park was, ordered a pizza and booked a cabin, night had come down. A dog raised its leg nonchalantly against the base of one of the old trees which spread their giant arcs over the street and a street light glinted off the statue of some long-dead pioneer as the dented Ford nosed its way up the hill. The faces at the windows of the Continental Hotel were fleshy slats against yellow glass, glimpsed through slim-line blinds which were new since the night he'd heard the liquid chimes of the clock striking midnight while the girl's breath sobbed beneath him.

The phone went off and he grabbed it up. He'd shoot the shit with Baz, talk about old times, ask how the business was, tell him yeah, he was still at the timber yard but he was assistant manager now.

'I don't know where you are,' the voice said, 'but when you get back I'll have your access rights revoked.'

'Fuck off!' The button on the phone killed her voice; he wished that it would kill her too.

As he unlocked the cabin door, he had the idea of turning the car round and driving and driving until he reached a place where white veils of heat drifted across the road and his eyelids were fattened by the sun. He put the pizza box down on the table and went out to get his daughter.

'Wakey, wakey, sweetheart.' He carried her in then wiped her face with a towel. He expected her to be whiny and querulous after her nap but she was quite composed. For dessert he'd bought a carton of strawberry ice cream and he watched her spoon it up carefully from the utilitarian white bowl.

'This has been a nice day,' she remarked conversationally, dabbing a tissue to her lips.

'Has it, princess? Has it?'

'Yes. A nice day.' Then, frowning slightly, as though the memory cost her effort and she had to find her way back to it: 'Are we going to see Mum tomorrow?'

'Yes.' He tamped down the lid of the carton firmly and stowed it in the fridge.

'And then you're coming back home with Mum and me?'

He opened his mouth to form some easy assurance but perhaps it was her searchlight gaze or the gratitude he felt for 'nice day'. Maybe it would never get any better than this for him, or for her. (Helen would keep the trophies dusted, he knew that.) Whatever the reason, he felt he owed her something real.

'No,' he said. 'Probably not.'

'But you'll come and visit?'

'Yes.'

'Good.' She kept eating, calmly enough, then put down her spoon and neatly wiped her mouth. 'Can I go on the swings now?'

'You don't think you'll be sick?' he teased.

'No.' She looked at him patiently, already a small survivor, a sturdy castaway from a shipwreck of adult life. Audrey: it was a funny, old-fashioned name to give a kid.

He took her hand and together they trudged through the dark to the sandpit in the far corner of the caravan park. In the orb of torchlight, balanced on the metal seat, with her hair tucked under a woolly hat, she looked like an ordinary little girl.

'Harder, Dad, harder!'

Her face flew out of focus then came back to him; as he held the light on her, her features smeared with joy. Back in the cabin, he'd wanted to say that he'd always be there, that he'd do anything for her, anything, but his nerve had failed. Promises were a bit like beauty: illusory, subject to change.

As he pushed his daughter higher, he had a sudden image of how he must appear, a dark figure looming at the edge of the wind, a form present but insubstantial, a white glare of face caught up in the crescendo of her happy scream, 'You're a ghost, Daddy! You're a ghost!'

Summer

She goes to the pool and swims in water heavy with a whole summer's detritus: Band-Aids, dead leaves and solitary earrings. A fine veil of dirt undulates at the bottom, stirred up by the kicking above. It's hot and no one will sleep tonight. She swims and swims in the sharp blue water then lies on her back and watches the boys down the deep end doing bombs. Look at me, look at me, they yell, then they hit the water. There's been a festival in the street outside and when she pushes open the exit door she smells roast meat on spits and almost collides with a woman wearing a headscarf, shepherding children. She starts to apologise but the woman looks at her blankly and hurries on. The stall holders are closing up and one of them calls hey you, girl, you want cake? He holds out a small cardboard box. Fifty cent. He thrusts the box at her. Here, here, I give to you. She eats as she walks, chewing up the sweet, greasy layers of pastry, rolling honey and gritty nuts around her tongue. The night is soft with heat and all along the street dark-eyed men lounge on verandahs while high, keening music pours out of the houses behind them and jasmine spirals from trellises. The men look at her as they go past but they don't say anything, they just watch her while the smoke from their cigarettes rises heavenwards. She turns into a quiet street and sees the car in front of her house, with a dark blockish head at the wheel. Fear dances like an acrobat along her spine until she looks again and then she rushes over and puts sugar-smeared lips on hers.

Vermin

The first time we done it, we done it for a joke. It was Craigie's idea. We went down to the dunny in the park one night and waited until one of 'em came along. Simmo and me held him while Craigie put the boots in and when we left him he was curled up on the ground, moanin' like a woman.

Craigie stood over him and spat. Fuck you, faggot, he says, be a while before ya come lookin' for another bum chum.

Then we got out of there. Fast. We seen him a few days later in the bookshop where he worked, all Yes, madam and No, madam in his fucken yellow vest. One of his eyes was purple and a yellow that matched the vest. We fucken cacked ourselves.

It got to be a bit of a habit up until grand final night. We drank a shitload of cans on the way to the match and then tried to sneak some through the gate, but it was no go; the poofta taking the tickets looked in our bags.

Ya gunna drink 'em all yaself, ya fucking spastic cunt? Simmo yelled over his shoulder.

Piss off, fat boy, the bloke at the gate says and Simmo turns around ready to go him but then we see Brett McKenna and the boys come out of the club rooms wearin' the old red and blue.

Go, Brett! Go, mate! we yelled. Come on the mighty Gulls!

And big Brett, he didn't let us down, soarin' above the rest like a hawk, like an eagle. It was all Brett all the way and the other side never had a chance.

It was over by three-quarter time and when the final siren sounded people started streamin' onto the ground. Some of the fellas had big Brett on their shoulders and were singin' the club song.

You're a legend! You're a legend! Simmo kept yellin' and even Craigie was grinning fit to beat the band.

Me, I just had my hands out tryin' to touch him. I would have done anything for him, then.

After the players went into the club rooms we hung around, pervin' at chicks. A blonde piece with really big norks went past.

Hey, tits! calls Simmo, pointin' at his dick. How about it?

Piss off, you pack of morons, she says, really pissed off, and then Simmo runs up behind her and grabs her arse.

We fucken cacked ourselves.

We got sicka hangin' around so after a while we piled into Craigie's Cruiser and hit the Royal.

My shout, I tell 'em, and head for the bar.

Wayne Preston, the half full-forward for the Gulls, is there.

Great game, mate! I say, but the cunt just looks straight through me. Fuck him.

We start drinkin' and keep drinkin', getting really shit-faced until, just before closing time, Craigie says, Let's go and find a faggot.

We all start poundin' the table. Find a faggot! Find a faggot! Let's go find a faggot!

Out the front of the pub there're cars revvin' and people yellin' – fucken spastic! – but when we get to the park it's as quiet as a grave and black as sin. There's no moon and someone's smashed the dunny light. We creep into the shadows to wait and pretty soon we hear footsteps. Craigie steps out.

You lookin' for something, mate? the poof says and there's the sound of someone unzipping his fly.

Yeah, this, says Craigie and then it's on for young and old.

Die, faggot, die! yells Simmo.

He was strong – who would have thought a fag could be so strong – he fought like a fucken tiger and even when Craigie kicked his teeth in he didn't cry or moan.

That'll teach the cunt a lesson and we hung a wheelie and took off outta there. He was all right when we left, just lyin' there in a puddle of blood.

The next mornin' the whole town's gotta hangover and I just stuff around feedin' the dogs and watchin' telly. I don't think nothin' about it till Simmo rings me first thing Monday.

Troy, Troy, have ya seen the paper, mate?

Course I haven't seen the friggin' paper but I go out for it because Simmo sounds cactus, he sounds really fucken scared, and there on the front page is the headline: 'Footy Hero Slain in Mystery Killing', and underneath, in fucken black and white: Brett McKenna dead at the hand of person or persons unknown.

'This is it?' Gina gazed uneasily out the window.

'This is it, babe.'

On the left-hand side, behind the dense banks of scrub that lined the road, the sea roiled in a sullen grey-blue mass and looked nothing like a postcard. A few salt-stunted trees bravely defied the wind, their tops flattened by years of exposure to storms and squalls. I shivered. Marcus had said the place could be bleak.

'Keep an eye out for the motel,' I told Gina as we came to the sign bearing the name of the town and, underneath, the number of friendly people who welcomed us.

We drove along the main street where harried-looking shoppers bent their heads down into the wind. A few people turned to stare at the Sharkmobile.

'There it is.' Gina pointed to a sign that flashed 'Four Seasons' in pink neon against the dark grey clouds but the first and last letters were on their way out and blinked intermittently: our season looked as though it was winter.

'Mrs Weatherall?' asked the young woman at the reception desk.

'Ms,' I replied curtly.

'Miss,' she said, beaming benignly. 'Please sign here.'

I signed, took the key and went outside to the car as my mobile rang.

'Lauri Weatherall.'

'It's Marcus, Lauri.'

I repressed a sigh. I was already regretting the impulse that had caused me to agree to his request at 5 a.m. yesterday morning. I'd been half asleep when he'd rung, with Gina, warm and smelling of roses, curled up next to me. I was weak. I hadn't had breakfast. I said 'Yes'.

'Let's meet at Café Pelican. It's not far from where you're staying and it's the only place in this dump where you can get soy milk lattes.'

Soy milk lattes, soy milk lattes, who gave a shit about soy milk lattes, but I said, 'Yeah, sure, see you in fifteen.'

Gina had the bags out of the car and was standing in front of the door numbered 9.

'Gotta dash, darl. I'll see you later,' after I'd parked the Sharkmobile. On the way out, I glanced at it longingly but thought that I'd do the right thing and walk.

I couldn't see any pelicans but a few seagulls foraged on the nature strips, pale yellow eyes alert for suitable refuse. The café was a cheery, hippy-looking place with a replica of its namesake out the front and wooden tables and chairs painted primary colours. Marcus cut a natty figure in paisley-patterned vest, dark shirt and yellow tie. We kissed, exchanged greetings and ordered.

'So tell me about this dead footballer.'

It took me a while to get the whole story: he kept looking around and lowering his voice but eventually it all came out. A 'family man' found where he shouldn't be, a spate of violent bashings and people frightened and intimidated. As he spoke, his hands clenched and unclenched and a blush mounted in his cheeks.

I looked at him closely. 'It happened to you, didn't it?'

He nodded miserably. 'The police said they'd look into it but I didn't hear from them again. You're my last hope, Lauri. I don't want anyone else getting killed.'

'How well did you know Brett McKenna?'

'Everyone "knew" Brett McKenna. When you're a small-town

footy hero, you're like God. But there were rumours; word gets around among the queers in a place as small as this.'

I bet it did. I wondered if Brett McKenna knew how vulnerable he had been. I drummed my fingers on the table and thought about my commitments back in the Big Smoke. I thought about grief and guilt. 'All right. I'll look into it.'

I made my farewells as he left some notes on the table. A gust of wind caught at my clothes as I stepped outside. Across the street an old derro swigged from a bottle in a brown paper bag. What a great place to be gay, I thought; where Saturday night entertainment probably meant Tabaret and Neil Diamond tribute bands and men grew up to marry their best friend's sister. I shuddered and high-tailed it back to the motel where Gina had filled the spa bath, picked a rose from one of the ailing bushes outside the reception office, and floated the petals on the water. I sank beneath it with relief. She'd done some research of her own.

'This is the place where the dolphins play.'

'Excuse me?' I nuzzled her neck.

'The dolphins. They come here to mate in the spring.'

I made diving movements with one of my hands. She giggled, took the hand, put it between her legs and moaned, just as my mobile, which was sitting on the tiles near the bath, rang. She made a completely different sound when I answered it but there was no one there. Must have been a wrong number; I went back to playing dolphins.

Next morning I visited the local police station and asked to speak to the senior officer. I was told that Senior Sergeant Winston had an RDO and could anyone else help.

'What's his first name?'

'Wally,' replied the young constable behind the counter. 'Hey, wait a minute...' but I was already out the door.

'Winston, W.' was listed in the phone book at an out-of-town address. I put the keys in the Sharkmobile and drove Gina and her credit cards to the town centre – she was raised Catholic but her real religion is shopping – then consulted a map of the district. As I took the road out of town, my mobile rang again but there was no one there.

Wally Winston was a big man nearing retirement age with a bent nose and very pale blue eyes. When I drove up, he was standing in his front yard polishing a big white diesel-powered ute. Angus cattle grazed placidly in the nearby paddocks. He took my proffered hand reluctantly and frowned when I told him I was a freelance journalist investigating the bashings. 'You're a long way from home.'

'I'm a friend of someone local.' I tried for a pleasant smile.

'Yeah? Well, you know what they say…' He smiled and the effect wasn't pleasant at all. 'You're only a local if your grandparents were born here.'

There didn't seem to be any reply to that so I pressed on with my business. When I mentioned the bashings, he looked non-committal.

'We investigated those. We couldn't find anything to substantiate the allegations.'

'The allegations? One man was in hospital for three days!'

'We know why they go there.' He leant against the side of his truck. 'They've only got themselves to blame.'

I thought about Marcus, lonely and closeted in a small conservative community and Brett McKenna who had died because he lived a lie.

'Everyone has the right to justice.' My words came out sounding more pompous than I intended.

He looked at me out of his pale blue eyes. 'They're just vermin. Disease-carrying vermin.'

As I drove away down the drive, I glanced in the rear-view mirror. He was standing watching me, arms folded. I was glad to get out onto the road. My mobile went off again and this time I heard breathing.

'Who is this?' But there was just the faint shallow breathing.

I threw the phone down and contemplated my next move. Clearly I was not going to get any further with the police. It was time to visit the wife.

On Tuesday morning, me'n Simmo took the greyhounds to the beach. They love it down there. We put 'em in Simmo's old station wagon and drove out of town to this quiet spot where we can run 'em up and down the beach with no idiots gettin' in the way. Thimble, the grey one, started actin' up and I put my head on her head and stoked it. Steady, girl. The waves were crashin' and the sun had come up like a big fried egg as I got down one end of the beach and Simmo got down the other and we ran the dogs between us, up and back, up and back. Bullseye flew across the sand like a black arrow and I thought how great dogs are because dogs aren't like people. Dogs don't disappoint you, dogs never let you down.

When we finished, we put 'em back in the car then leant against it and had a smoke.

Whatta we gunna do? Simmo asks and I know he's not talkin' about the dogs.

I take a deep drag of me smoke. No one saw us do nothin', I say at last. We should just try not t'think about it, but I know that's easier sad that done.

All through the week I have dreams about blood and slime and on Sunday night the phone rings and it's Craigie sayin' some real butch type's been snoopin' around, askin' questions and makin' a real fucken nuisance of herself. A real bull dyke.

But when he starts tellin' me what she looks like, I say, Yeah, yeah, cause I've seen her drivin' round in her big fucken tank of a car; drivin' round with her girlfriend sittin' up beside her like king dick – not that she'd have one, ha, ha! The girlfriend's not bad-looking in a woggy sort of way, long wavy dark hair and norks out to here. I never seen any lezzos before except in porn mags, two sheilas doing flash the gash stuff.

We could teach her a lesson, Craigie says, and I say, Hey, steady on, 'cause I know what Craigie's like. He can be a real mad bastard. His dad use t'beat him with chains and when his mum left home, she didn't take Craigie with her.

We've gotta keep a low profile, I tell 'im, and t'change the subject I ask, How do ya reckon lesos do it?

Probably use falsies, he says. Great big fucken rubber ones they buy at sex shops, and we fucken cack ourselves.

Chez McKenna was a large, split-level brick veneer with a neat and tidy garden. The windows were shuttered with apricot-coloured Kosta blinds. Karin McKenna was a slim, small-featured blonde wearing jeans and a crisp white shirt – everything neat and clean and nice. She was probably about thirty but today she looked older. I'd rung and told her I was a reported from a footy magazine – *Marks and Matches* – and wanted to do a profile on Brett which emphasised the community-building aspects of sport. She showed me into a lounge room which had apricot-coloured carpet and paler walls. A blonde boy and girl smiled from framed photographs on the coffee table.

'Nice kids,' I said, after I'd given my condolences.

'Sherrine and Jordan,' she said and for a moment her face relaxed.

It was a good opening for an interview and I took advantage. I learned that she and Brett had been childhood sweethearts – her brother Garry was Brett's best mate – and that they'd married young. She told me – it was one of those weird ironies of life – that Brett had had offers from big city clubs but had decided to stay in the town because he and Karin thought it was a good place to bring up kids. Brett's job as a sales rep for a big agricultural fertiliser company had flexible hours and allowed plenty of time for training. They'd been happy.

'You didn't resent the time footy took him away from his family?'

She smiled. 'How could I, when it meant so much to him?'

I turned back to the photos. One showed Brett, blokey and handsome, wearing a football jumper. Who would have guessed he'd gone to public toilets to have sex with other men? Karin saw me looking and for a moment her face blazed with anger. Not just anger: it was the look of a woman betrayed. She'd known about his secret, or at least guessed, but she had never been able to tell anyone, not even herself. I thanked her, said I would send her a copy of the finished article and went outside to a day where the sun had finally decided to shine.

Two young boys stood inspecting the Sharkmobile. One was stroking a tail fin. 'Cool car,' he said, by way of greeting.

'Thanks. It's a 1960 Chevrolet Bel Air. It was an American-designed car but there were some right-hand drives assembled in Oz, back in the days when we had a car industry.' As I opened the door, I noticed someone up the street, watching me. An old guy, bundled in clothes against the sharp wind, with a shuffling walk and silver hair. 'Who's that?' I asked, pointing.

'That's just old Lou. Lou McSwain.'

'I've seen him before.'

'He hangs around,' snickered the other kid. 'Usually in the pub or the park.'

'He's an alkie,' volunteered the first, cupping his hand and raising it to his mouth.

'He used to be a teacher,' said the second. 'But then he started drinking. Big time.' He mimicked his friend's gesture.

Now I remembered. I'd seen the old man outside the café the day I'd arrived. So he liked to wander around. I gave a mental shrug. 'Thanks, fellas.'

'Check ya.' The first raised his hand magisterially as he and his mate moved off.

Lou McSwain had disappeared.

I stood by the car ordering my thoughts. I had run up against a wall of silence and no one was going to help me. What next? A languid cappuccino with my darling appealed but I needed to clear my head: a solitary walk was required. The beach was on the other side of a caravan park a few streets away. I could get the car on the way back. I set off, thinking that this walking was getting to be a bad habit.

The caravan park had the usual kiosk and phone box as well as a few people making the most of the sun. A section of natural vegetation had been left at the rear of the park; a track cut through the scrub, leading to the sand and water. As I started down the track, my mobile rang. There was the same rapid shallow breathing then a faint voice.

'We have to meet…'

'Why?'

'I know things…'

'Where?'

'Just keep walking. I'll meet you on the beach.' The caller hung up.

The sun went behind a cloud and I realised how quiet it was. A twig snapping made me start and although I couldn't see anyone when I looked around I quickened my pace. There was another sound, closer this time, and the hair on the back of my neck rose. I've learned never to distrust these primeval reactions; I was certain I was being followed.

I stopped and turned. 'Who's there?'

There was only silence. Fragments of sunlight reached through a black lattice of branches as I broke into a jog. Had the big cop disliked me enough to want to hurt me? The caller might have rung from the caravan park. Perhaps I was being set up by a murderer. There was the sound of someone crashing through scrub and I ran. The waves were louder now but so were the footsteps behind me. An arm went around my throat. I saw red before my eyes. A voice shouted something and then the world fell on me.

I woke up in a hospital bed with a small, silver-haired man sitting next to it.

I get a phone call and it's the dyke sayin', Meet me in the aquarium. What the fuck? I nearly decide not to show but I want t'see what she knows so I go down to the beach to the big fucken pile of rocks where the aquarium is. It's underground, really fucken dark and creepy. There's water in puddles on the floor and a drip, drip, drip that's the only sound. I check out the fish while I wait, little stripy black and yella ones, big old crays, and an octopus crawlin' around on the bottom of its tank. I knock on the glass and when it waves an arm at me I wave back. In the biggest tank there's this shark. It's only a little shark but you can see its real mean teeth and its real mean eyes, cold as the sea in winter. I stand there watchin' it swim around and around but I don't want to t'go any closer.

I'm gettin' bored, gettin' ready to go, then I feel someone behind me and when I turn around, there she is. Watchin'.

G'day, I'm…

Yeah, I know who you are, she says, real snotty like. Bitch.

There's glass at the top of the aquarium to let in the light and it makes weird strips on the stone floor like the stripes on the fucken fish while she looks at me from behind her shades and doesn't say nothin'.

Why d'ya pick this place? I say at last.

To look at the fish, and she gives me this weird fucken little smile and starts ravin' on about her car, how it's a shark, it's her Sharkmobile and she like cruisin' in it.

I think about that good-lookin' chick of hers and say something about the back seat havin' a lotta room and she laughs and says, Yeah, it does.

We talk about cars and I tell her about goin' to the speedway and watchin' the drag racing, how it's a real fucken buzz and she says, Yeah, it would be.

We talk a bit more and I'm startin' to think she's all right for a leso, then right outta the fucken blue she asks me about Brett McKenna. Did I know 'im? Did I know anything about the murder, and where was I that night? I play it real dumb and say I was in the pub with everyone else till closin' time, then I went home.

That's not what I've heard, she says, and I give her this big, shit-eating grin and say she musta heard wrong.

She just looks at me from behind the shades and doesn't say nothin', while the shark swims around and around, bumpin' its nose against the glass. She looks at it real thoughtful and mutters something about predators and victims.

Can I go now, miss? I ask, cheeky, as though I'm talkin' to Miss

Johnson, the old bag who use t'give me the cuts in primary school, and she just gives me this vacant sorta nod, not lookin' at me, as though she's got somethin' on her mind. Hey, Troy! She calls after me as I head towards the steps. A man always kills the thing he loves. She gives this weird fucken funny little laugh, and I get outta there. Fast.

'How did you get my mobile number?' I asked and he smiled shyly and said I wasn't the only detective. He was probably younger than he looked; years of alcohol and living rough had taken their toll. He was well-spoken, with the refined, English-type accent that I associate with old-style ABC newsreaders. I wondered what had brought him this low. His eyes were bloodshot and his hand shook but he seemed sober as he told me what he'd seen the night Brett McKenna died. The moon had come out briefly. He'd got a good look at one face.

'Would you make a statement?'

'Yes. People shouldn't suffer like that.' His face opened briefly. I caught a glimpse of some old unhealed wound.

My mouth framed a question; then I decided against it. 'Thanks for rescuing me.'

He smiled. 'Think nothing of it.' He'd followed me from Karin McKenna's and, when he'd seen where I was heading, made a call from the phone box and followed me into the bush. If he hadn't been there, I have ended up with far more than a bump on the head and bruising. Two men had attacked me; one face was a match for who he'd seen the night of the murder.

After Lou McSwain left, I sat in bed thinking about the choices we make and how people can live out their lives in silence until it destroys them.

Gina collected me the next day. I was sore and needed more rest but knew that the more time passed, the harder it would be to find someone who fitted the description Lou McSwain had given me. Still, there couldn't be too many young men with red hair and a spider tattoo on their neck in a town this size. Could there?

'That sounds like Troy Harris,' Gerard, the young constable I'd spoken to on my previous visit, told me when I called in at the station. He'd arrested Harris twice, for vandalism and petty theft. 'He keeps bad company, that one.'

It wasn't hard to track Troy Harris down and as soon as I saw him I knew all about the poor sad little son-of-a-bitch. Born in a backwater of genetically impoverished stock, his dad had pissed off early, leaving mum to go it alone. This, combined with impatient teachers, inadequate education and declining job prospects in rural areas had all made Troy a bored stupid young man with low self-esteem. Lou McSwain had seen three men attack Brett McKenna; Troy wouldn't have done it alone. He was like one of Hitler's innumerable henchmen who were 'just following orders'. No, there would have been a leader, someone born cruel or made cruel by the world.

I had to let Troy go at the aquarium but after he'd gone I stood there leaning against the shark's tank, listening to the relentless drip, drip, drip of the water and looking at the table covered in tacky little dolphin souvenirs: dolphin pencil sharpeners, dolphin fridge magnets, dolphins which doubled as both… I had doubts about Lou McSwain making a statement. Even if he didn't change his mind, the word of a semi-itinerant alcoholic was unlikely to carry much weight in court. I climbed up the stairs and trudged back to the Sharkmobile. The sun was going down, throwing harsh gold light onto the waves as it sank beneath them. I wound down the window and drove back to the motel with the breeze in my hair, thinking that there was only one thing for it. It would have to be the boy and I'd have to break him.

Last night I had the weirdest fucken dream. I'm in the water, deep down in the sea and it's real bright blue, fulla light and beautiful. I'm swimmin' around, lookin' at the light shinin' down through the water, swimmin' and swimmin', but then there are clouds, shadows, above. I look up and all I can see is these big pale bellies blockin' out the light. I can't see nothin' else but then there's blood, great big streams of blood, swirlin' all though the water and I see that the big pale things are sharks come after the blood. It's Brett's blood; there's his arms and legs turnin' over like some great big fucken sacrifice. The sharks come nearer and nearer, nosin' through the water and I can see their big fucken teeth and suddenly, I know it's not Brett they're after, it's me. It's punishment for what I done.

Ya see, I knew it was Brett standin' there that night: me mum's always said I've got eyes like a hawk and just for a second the moon came out from behind the clouds and I seen him. I shoulda stopped it. I coulda stopped it, somehow stepped in fronta Craigie and made out we was doin' it for a joke. Hey, Brett, how's it goin' mate. Fancy a bit of me arse? And we coulda all hadda laugh and gone home. But, once Craigie started kickin' him, I had t'join in and, once I started, I couldn' stop.

So it's my fault he's dead. In the dream, the sharks are closin' in an' the water's boilin' with blood. Bits of hand and arm float past me like some sicko horror movie. Brett's eyes, one hundred metres up, look at me like they did the night he died.

I woke up screamin' and sweatin' then lay there lookin' out the little winda of me bedroom, thinkin' about the dogs and who's gunna take care of 'em, cause that leso's onto me. She's out there cruisin' in her big fucken Sharkmobile and she's comin' to get me.

The Meeting

The girl stands in front of the mirror, tugging down the thin jumper. It's brown with white stripes and she knows it's no good. She has big saggy tits which drag the stripe down and make them pucker and curve. She stands there, makes a face in the mirror, then goes into the kitchen where her father sits with the paper in front of the unlit wood stove. So what's it gunna be like, this meeting? I don't know, just a meeting. There gunna be people there jumpin up and down, shoutin praise de lawd? I don't know, says the girl. Don't know, don't know, what do ya know? Not a lot, says the girl and she walks down the front path, past rows of beans and cabbages neat as braided hair.

While she waits, she thinks about the half-dark hall, all the singing and crying and calling out to Jesus. (Jesus ain't no lover for a woman.) The caterwauling and bawling and upturned faces. Eva Pearson rolling on the floor with her dress pulled up under the pastor's moon-faced gaze.

The girl tugs down her jumper and listens for the car. The boy's late but she knows he'll turn up; they've had this arranged for a week.

There's a sound like distant thunder and when the old puke-green Ford with the foxtail hanging from its antenna comes round the corner she grips the top of the gate so tightly flakes of rust come away in her hands. He's got a half-bottle of Jim Beam and when she hands it back the neck's ringed with brown smudges and sweat. She's seen him driving down the main street on Friday night, one hand on the steering wheel and the other on the can between his legs. She doesn't know why he comes to the meetings, she only knows that when they saw Eva Pearson on the floor their eyes met and he smirked.

After the meeting they sat out in the car while people called out cheerfully, you behave yourselves now, before going back to conversations about the Holy Spirit and the price of fencing wire. He kept looking at his hands and shifting around in his seat while she asked him about the footy team and how many wins they'd had. Not many, they were playing shit house, and then he apologised for using language. He had a sweet face and smelt of Brut 33 and yes, she thought, he'll do.

At home, she brought up his family's name, just casually, and her father put down his paper and stared. You going round with those tall Irish boys? You better watch yourself, girl.

The girl watched herself: she watched herself in the mirror and in the meetings and afterwards in the car. She sat on the hard wooden seats in the hall watching people open their mouths and utter dark streams of words which rose up to Jesus and wondered what it was like.

When he stops the car in the clearing, he hands her the bottle again but she shakes her head. She doesn't want to be like the girls she reads about in *Truth*: 'He drugged me then took advantage…' or 'Girl, sixteen, sold into degradation'. He leans towards her and she cups the hot mystery of his breath in her mouth, tastes liquor and smells cheap aftershave. When he tips the seat back, she knows he's done this before and she's glad.

Their voices rise, grappling and calling, past the dark trees, while she straddles him awkwardly and he fumbles with his zipper and swears. She expects pain but there isn't any and as she rides him her power rises like sap. Wild hallelujahs burst from her throat while he puts his hands on those heavy tits and moans as if he's receiving a sacrament or a blow. He's saying words she can't hear, begging slow down, slow down but he doesn't know she's got a dervish inside. Scarlet arpeggios leap from her and she opens to him like a flower, like a Venus flytrap while he howls in adoration below. She milks him and drinks him, tasting his sweet blood while his eyes roll back in his head and he clamours to be saved. He's moaning, he's begging, there's a sea of fire around them and when he cries oh-christ-god-jesus she blesses him and they glide, clear-eyed and sanctified, through to the other side.

On the way back, she tries to talk but he won't look at her, he only grunts and drops her at the corner instead of driving right up to the gate.

The girl feels a flash of contempt but it passes and when she gets out she thanks him and gently closes the door. Branded, she thinks, watching the red gimlet eyes recede. The devil's spawn. The empty bottle hits the road and explodes into fragments of light. She starts walking.

When she reaches the house, she creeps in so she doesn't wake the others. The sky's clear and night light burnishes the old wood and worn lino. The girl takes down the big white enamel bowl with the dark blue rim, fills it from the kitchen tap and gets a thin rough towel from the cupboard in the hallway. She stands over the bowl and laves herself, ladling cool water between her thighs while she watches the tendrils of blood curl in the bowl and disappear.

After she washes away the blood and stink, she dries herself with the towel, rubs herself so hard the skin mottles and streaks. She picks up the heavy bowl, carries it carefully to the yard and tips red-tinged water onto the plants. Then she goes inside and rinses and dries the bowl. Still holding the towel, she moves quietly down the hall, and stands outside her brothers' room. Now you be a mother to them, her mother had whispered in the hospital but the girl didn't need to be told. She tiptoes in and strokes the hair of the littlest. They remind her of something she's seen in the window of the second-hand shop in town, the row of rotund wooden dolls with painted cheeks, which fit snugly, one inside the other.

When she reaches her room, she turns down the blankets and crawls under. Faint blue bruises bloom across her breasts, she feels a familiar soreness and knows that soon she will bleed. No drama, she thinks. In the morning she'll be up with sun to get the boys off to school and will watch the bus raise the plumes of dust as it ambles along the road. Her father will come into the kitchen wanting bacon and eggs and start yakking about the meeting. Who fell over, go on, you tell me. Did that silly old bugger Jackie Merton fall over? The girl sighs but then the lines on her face ease: no use wishing for something you don't have.

Through the uncurtained window she sees stars and the dense familiar outline of trees. She falls asleep beneath the dark mantle of sky.

Little Sheilas

She was nine, with skinny colt legs and a body hard and brown as a stick.

'Little sheilas,' muttered Elsie O'Brien, wiping hands like plates of meat on a tea towel and taking a cup and saucer from the cupboard. 'Little sheilas,' watching the girl as she came dripping out of the dam, naked except for a pair of faded cotton shorts. 'Little sheilas,' pulling out her copy of *True Confessions* and settling down to read until the girl came padding into the kitchen, hair still damp and shoulders lightly scourged with sunburn.

The girl put down the small canvas bag, took the chocolate box from the bench and sat down at the end of the kitchen table.

'Would you like some cordial?'

'Yes.'

'Yes, what?'

'Yes, please,' said the girl, without looking up. She was taking the horses out of the box, frowning slightly, and arranging them on the table.

'That's a new one.' There was a dark blue horse with bunched and rolling muscles and a mane and tail covered in silver foil which had come out of Else's pantry.

'That's *The Ghost*. I drew him last week.'

'I didn't know you got blue horses,' said Else, with an edge of malice.

'You can,' said the girl patiently. 'They're called blue roans.'

'And I've never seen a horse with a silver mane and tail.'

'Shut up,' said the girl. 'I read it in a book.'

'Oh, then it must be right.' Else lumbered over to the stove to put the kettle on, grunting like an old horse herself. Her veins were giving her buggery today but what could you expect when you'd pushed out seven of your own. She took the Kia-Ora and the ice blocks from the fridge and sloshed them into a glass which she filled from the tap.

The girl opened one of the books, *Wild Horses of the West*, and took up the tracing paper and pencil. There was a furiously galloping brown mustang which she wanted for the box.

Little sheilas, thought Elsie O'Brien, reaching for the packet of butternut snaps. The girl was always there, at the end of the table, cutting and pasting and colouring. A strange way to carry on but what could you expect from a kid who had the snobs at the top of the hill for parents? Else held up the packet, trying to remember when it had been opened, then plonked down half a dozen biscuits on a flower-patterned plate. The girl had almost finished tracing; there were small tears in the paper where she had dug in too hard. -

'Drink your drink.'

The kettle on the stove began to shriek.

'In a minute.' The girl transferred the tracing to the cover of an old exercise book and began going over the flaring nostrils and flattened ears. She slid the pencil down the rump then around the clattering hooves then looked at Else for the first time, pushed the book away and picked up her drink. She tasted it, made a face then went over to the fridge for more cordial.

'You gunna tell me a story?'

'In a minute.'

'Think I'll rename you "In-a-minute-Peterson".' Else parked her huge behind on a chair and gently pushed the teapot back and forth. '"In a minute I'll do this", "In a minute I'll do that". People like you, they spend so much time rushin' around, they never get a minute to do anything.'

The girl looked at Else over the rim of her glass.

'Be kind to the old girl,' her stepfather had told her. 'She's had a hard life.'

The girl's mother, turning away from the sideboard with the drinks in her hand, snorted. 'Some people make their own hardship.'

'What's the matter, Caroline? You don't want her fraternising with the locals?'

'Oh, fraternising, yes, fraternising.'

Most days now, after school, the girl stopped off at Else's, plunging into the dam on the way. She was a good swimmer but had a horror of her toes touching all the life she imagined wriggling and oozing in the mud at the bottom. She lay on her back looking up at the hard blue dome of the sky, feeling the silty brown water lap her body and soothe the bloody scrapes on her knees. Then she clambered out and ran the rest of the way as fast as she could so that by the time she burst into the cool green kitchen she was dizzy and white light danced before her eyes. It was a test to make herself stronger and she would sit there catching her breath, waiting for the slashes of light to disappear before she started colouring and cutting and pasting, all of which was a dress rehearsal for the moment she picked up the horses and began.

'There was once a proud blue roan stallion called The Ghost…'

'Just a minute, love. Gotta get myself a little something.' Else ambled over to the cupboards and took down the bottle.

The girl had been expecting this and waited until Else poured some of the fumey brown liquid into her tea, then began again.

'There was once a mighty stallion called The Ghost who lived in a high wide valley near the sea. He was very beautiful, with a dark blue coat and a silver mane and tail which flowed like moonlight. Stories of his beauty and strength had spread far and wide and many men had tried to capture and tame him but to no avail.'

'Avail,' said Elsie O'Brien, savouring the word like a heavy dark plum and reaching for the bottle again.

'Ssshhh!' said the girl. 'Sometimes at night The Ghost would leave his safe valley and thread his way down to the sea, his hooves striking sparks from the granite rocks which lined the high cliffs. When he reached the beach, he would gallop along the hard white sand, with the moon casting crescents of light upon the water and the waves crashing like dull thunder. The sky was dark but bright and The Ghost moved like a shadow, his coat blending perfectly with the night. He galloped and galloped until he was exhausted and then he started for home, stopping to crop the lush green grass along the way, tired and footsore but with his coat streaked with starlight.'

'Well, that's lovely, love.' Else helped herself to the bottle then topped up her cup with tea. 'But he does sound kind of lonely. Aren't you gunna give him a little girlfriend? Like in here?' She pointed to the *True Confessions* and sniggered.

'No,' said the girl firmly. 'Horses don't think like that.'

Little sheilas, thought Elsie O'Brien tenderly. Little sheilas, not all messed up. Not all messed with love and stuff.

'I'm gunna tell you a story. I'm gunna tell you a story that'll knock ya socks off.'

'Not yet. I haven't finished.' The girl's eyes narrowed to greenish slits.

The girl dug around in the bottom of the cardboard box until she found two plastic cowboys taken from a packet of cereal. She placed them on the table and continued.

'One day two men came to the mountain looking for The Ghost. They had made a bet with their friends, for a lot of money, that they would capture and tame him. The men were cunning and patient and had taken their best stock horses with them. They spent many days tracking The Ghost without success but one morning they caught sight of him returning from one of his nocturnal jaunts…'

'Jaunts!' snickered Else. 'Nocturnal jaunts! Which book didja get that from?' She half-slumped onto the table, resting her weight on her forearms and stared balefully at the girl.

'With a fierce yell, the men wheeled their horses around and gave chase. The Ghost, realising he was being pursued, broke into a gallop, weaving through the trees in the hope that he could elude them. But he was already tired…'

'From his nocturnal jaunt?' interposed Else.

'…and they rode horses which were fit and fresh. The Ghost raced through the trees, making for more densely timbered country through which ran a narrow but swiftly flowing stream. Sweat streaked his coat and foam gathered at the corners of his mouth; his breath came in great rasping gasps as the men drew closer. Terror gripped The Ghost, terror that he would be captured…'

'He didn't stand a ghost of a chance?' snickered Else.

'…and made to wear a saddle and bridle and forced to carry a hated man on his back. He would rather die than live like that! He would rather die!' The girl looked up for a moment. She was breathing quickly and her pupils had dilated so much her eyes looked almost black.

'Steady on, love, steady on. Don't burst a blood vessel. There's worse things in life, you know,' Else giggled. She pushed the plate of butternut snaps towards the girl. 'Here, have another bickie. Would you like a ginger nut instead?'

The girl picked up the blue horse and moved him further along the table, with the two men standing by. 'Down, down the steep slope The Ghost galloped, with his flanks heaving and stones flying from underneath his hooves. He swerved suddenly as he felt the air near his ears move; the lasso, which one of the men had thrown, landed harmlessly against his rump. With his last ounce of strength, The Ghost launched himself into the river, which bore him swiftly away to safety. The men, thwarted, watched him from the river bank, cursing and beating the air…'

'Little sheilas,' muttered Elsie O'Brien sullenly. 'Little sheilas. Don't know the half of it. I could tell ya a story…'

'…they were beating the air with their fists. The water washed the sweat from The Ghost's matted coat and cleaned the dirt from his cut legs. It carried away the blood-streaked foam…'

'Hey, steady on, love. Steady on.'

'Be quiet, please. The Ghost let the kind water carry him along until he regained his strength. He staggered from the river, rolling in the thick grass and made his way back to the valley where he lived.'

'That's lovely, love.' Else propped herself on one elbow and reached for the bottle, then the teapot. Tea slopped over the lip of the cup and pooled in the saucer. 'Ya a born storyteller. Don't know where ya get it all from.'

'I make it all up,' lied the girl. Only some came out of her head; the rest was from the books which lined the shelves in her room, next to the computer and compact discs. The idea for the horses had come from an old book she had found when she and her mother were packing up the house in the city. She turned back to the embryo mustang. Come on, come on, she thought, knowing Else would soon get up to go to the toilet.

'What colour?'

'Eh?'

'What colour?' The girl pointed to the tracing. 'What colour should I do him?'

'Shit, I dunno. Colour him purple for all I care. 'Scuse me, love, 'scuse me, I've gotta…' Else stumbled in the direction of the lavvy.

As soon as she was gone the girl tiptoed out of the kitchen. It wasn't subterfuge which made her move so quietly, it was more a sense of occasion. The lounge room had a fusty smell of cheap brandy overlaid by air freshener and a large old-fashioned television squatted in one corner. On top of this and the dresser beside it, stood the clusters of photographs, showing wedding processions and smiling couples and tables of party goers.

Families fascinated the girl. Over the weeks, she had been able to piece whole histories together, who fitted with who and where the gaps and dead ends occurred. Her favourites were the moon-headed babies who stared out inquisitively. In a small black-and-white snapshot a heavy, dark-haired man squinted off to the side of the frame, next to a younger thinner Else. There was a series of colour photos, in which she wore a floral shift and a brassy helmet of hair and stood grouped with children, some carroty and freckled, some stocky and dark. The only trace of the man was in some of the square clumsy faces. They looked, the girl thought, like the kids who made fun of her accent – 'Dah-ance! Cha-ance!' – and who liked to trip her up at morning recess. Older versions of them grinned and preened in front of churches and twenty-first birthday cakes, wearing ugly wide-legged trousers and dresses which made her shudder. Weird stuff. Sometimes, when she stood in front of the photos she saw her face dimly reflected in the glass or cheap plastic sheathing, the top of her head and her eyes moving behind a row of satiny debutantes or a brocade-clad matron of honour, like a shadow moving under dirty water.

Down the hallway, the toilet flushed. Else came into the kitchen and found her leaning over the newly traced horse, red crayon in hand. The girl smelt the grog and something acrid underneath. She wanted to go herself but thought she'd wait until she got home; she didn't want to see the splashes on the seat. She picked up the new horse and placed him carefully on top of the pile in the chocolate box.

'What are you going to name him?' asked Else.

'I'll think about it tomorrow.' The girl looked out the window, where the first stars pricked the sky. Her mother would be taking the decanter from the sideboard and pouring drinks for herself and her husband. He would complain about the amount of soda with the whisky and her mother would tell him to get it yourself, your lordship.

The girl shivered and pulled on socks and pants and jumper. She pushed her feet into heavy brown sandals, placed her cap, peak slanting backwards, on her head and picked up the bag. 'Thanks for the biscuits and cordial,' she said politely. 'I'll see you tomorrow.'

'Yeah, love. It's nice to have a cuppa. Off ya go.'

The girl set off towards the big house on top of the rise. Her stepfather's horses grazed in the adjoining paddock but she hardly gave them a glance. The were a dull lot, bays and browns and one that was almost black, not like the glittering manes and tails and reds and oranges of the paper horses. On nights like this she liked to lie naked on top of the bedclothes, flying over the sea, her hair streaming behind her. She forgot about the hard wooden seats at the new school and the kids who lay in wait for her in the playground. She ran through the paddocks of tough stringy grass, cantered along beaches and when she slept she dreamt of white sand and white horses.

Else staggered to the window, bottle in hand, and watched her walk down the path into the gloom. The little arse on her, she thought, the little stride. Just like…ah, just like… A small sound escaped her and for a moment she saw her reflection in the flat black pane of glass. Oh, you old hooer, you poor battered old hooer. She put the bottle to her mouth and drank deeply, using the back of her hand to wipe away a trickle which escaped a corner and rolled down her chin. 'I'll tell you a story… I'll tell you a story'll knock ya socks off.' There was a dull red fog building up behind her eyes and through the window the stars gleamed pitilessly down.

'Little sheilas,' she muttered. 'Little sheilas,' and drew the curtains against the night.

Chris

He was a long-limbed boy with black hair and grey eyes and in summer his skin darkened to the colour of the crackling bark on trees. There was some talk about the father's family having a touch of blood, that the old man was really a quarter-caste and they took it out on the boy at school. It hurt him, the taunts of darkie and boong and he knew it wasn't fair, his younger brother blonde and brown-eyed and his sister freckly and mousey, no colour at all. He'd come home sometimes with a bloody nose and scraped knuckles and his father would look at him and say nothing.

He didn't see any point in staying on so when his fifteenth birthday came around, he left. You'll have to pull your weight, his father said, I don't want any bludgers around here, but Chris was a good worker. There was a dog he had, a mottled reddish thing which was deaf in one ear and every morning when the mist was still stuck to the trees and the spiders' webs strung with rain they'd go out in the dark for the cows. He'd be deep down in some dream in the room he shared at the back of the house with his brother then he'd wake to see his mother standing over him, her eyes black-fringed and her mouth a curved red sickle because even at six in the morning she'd be made up like a mad fairy princess. She'd shove a cup of tea and a slice of toast into his hands and after that he'd stumble out and call the dog, which trotted alongside him through the wet slush of grass.

It rained a lot there; sometimes the water would blur the blue shapes of trees looming through the dawn and the cows' breath make white clouds on the air. Chris did the whole hundred on his own, the spilt milk running in rivers through the mud and shit while the sun laved golden light across the grass and afterwards he'd go to the old stone trough for bucket after bucket of water. This was the part of the day he liked best, the concrete gleaming wetly and the cows slack-uddered and peaceful in the paddocks as he and dog trudged home.

Don't forget to wipe your feet, his mother would yell and then Chris would cook himself bacon and eggs and another stack of toast; sometimes he'd get through a whole tin of jam.

You're eating me out of house and home, boy, and he'd look up to see his father standing at the door, still dressed in pyjamas. I'm not made of money, you know. He'd stare at Chris for a while then he'd go to his room and get dressed. Later, you'd see him walking around, checking fences and looking at stock, narrowing those black eyes against the light.

Can I have some money, Dad? Chris asked at the end of the first month.

I'll give it to you when you're eighteen, and then it was I'll give it to you when you're twenty-one.

There was an old car left to rust in a patch of bush next to the farm and sometimes Chris would go and sit there, sit there for hours with the dog because he couldn't stand to hear his brother cry.

Andrew cried all the time, cried a scalding reservoir of tears from morning to night.

What's the matter, what's the matter, Chris asked but Andrew just cried and cried.

Their sister never did anything much, just sat with their mother cutting pictures from magazines and wishing she could marry some movie star.

Who'd have ya, ya lazy young hooer? their father would say. Ya wouldn't work in an iron lung, and then he'd go out to his shed.

Their mother had a pair of scissors that she loved, gold, in the shape of a bird, and when Chris sat in the car he'd watch the red badge of the parrot's wing, the perfect magpies and shiny crows and he'd think about her at the table. He'd make up stories in his head about what he'd do if he ever got away, the places he'd go and the things he'd see but mostly he looked at his own magazines, the pages of glossy tits and gleaming slits he'd spent his dole money on. He'd buy them at the only shop where he lived, which was run by a woman and her daughter. No one knew where they came from but they sold fruit and veg, ran a post office and there was a special little place at the back for the magazines.

Chris didn't mind getting them off the mother, a huge old thing with stringy hair, but one day it was the daughter looking slyly from behind the counter. I n-n-need a few things for Mum, stammered Chris. It's her birthday s-s-soon, and the girl smirked and pointed to a tall and hideous vase painted dark blue with tan flowers slashed on its side.

What am I meant to do with this? his mother said as she put it outside in the wash house.

Chris hadn't thought it was that bad.

You keep it, he said to the girl. You keep it. I don't want no money for it. What's ya name?

Gwennie, she said, and she smiled and pushed back her hair.

Suet pudding, he thought, when he first saw her naked, suet pudding, the pale mounds quivering and shaking. They used a room behind the shop and sometimes, when they'd finished, Chris would lie there and listen to the rain. Once, Gwennie said something about black babies and Chris hit her, hit her hard, although he was sorry afterwards and didn't like to see her cry.

It's all right, it's all right, Gwennie said. I'm not prejudiced or nothing.

Saturday nights they'd go to the pub and he'd stand at the bar with the other young blokes talking about footy and cows. Sometimes some hippies from the coast would come in with guitars and sing. They'd play old things like 'I Put A Spell On You' and 'Heart of Stone' and then their own terrible songs, full of words like 'universe' and 'meaningful'. Get off, ya pack of wombat rooters, someone would call and the hippies would pack their tribe of women and kids into a Kombi and go.

When Chris stood at the bar, he'd see Gwennie sitting at the table with the other girls, botting cigarettes from the one next to her and laughing fit to beat the band. He'd stare at her for a moment then down at the yellow dregs of his beer. I could go on like this for years.

When Chris was twenty-four, the old man on the next farm died. Who'll buy the place? City buggers, said the locals but then they heard that some bloke from upcountry had bought it and he came down driving a long red car. Bit of a flash bugger, but Archie O'Connell was all right. One morning in May he knocked on the door about a cow in trouble and Chris went to give him a hand.

Come on, girl, good girl. The cow was lying in a corner paddock with her eyes rolled back, a sheen of rain on her flanks and darker patches where the pain had come through. Come on, girl, good girl. They got her up and then they stayed there all day till they saw the first gelatinous hoof and the calf tumbled out, a quivering wet huddle of bones.

Slinks.

Beg yours?

Slinks. That's what they call them when they're born too young.

They watched it stagger to its feet, collapse then get up again, nose at the teats and guzzle.

You want to come and work for me? I've got more than I can handle.

Chris didn't say anything, just watched the tiny tail whisk back and forth.

I'll pay you, said Archie O'Connell.

I'll pay you, I'll pay you, repeated Chris, all the time it took him to walk home. I'll pay you, I'll pay you, slashing through the watery grass.

Archie's gunna pay me, and his father gave a laugh like plywood breaking in two. I'll believe it when I see it.

But Archie was as good as his word. In the evenings, after they'd finished, Chris didn't bother going home for a while. He'd have tea with Archie, then they'd sit in the lounge room and talk because Archie was an interesting bloke. He was pretty old, about fifty, and he'd done a lot of interesting things.

Women tried to help him when he first moved in, brought over casseroles and cakes, but Archie could cook and had fixed the place up for himself. He'd pinned a map of the world to the lounge room wall and he pointed out to Chris all the places he'd been with the merchant navy; and he'd grown wheat in the Wimmera, he'd owned another farm and he'd spent time training horses for the track. They'd yarn away for hours, drinking tea or having a few beers, with Archie sitting on the old red sofa and Chris by the fire in a chair. The flames would shine on the jug of daffodils and the glass-fronted cabinet where Archie kept his books. Old books, with shabby blue or maroon covers and written by people Chris had never heard of, except for Banjo Paterson and Shakespeare. You can borrow them if you like, but Chris mainly liked to hear Archie talk. He'd forget about Gwennie, who'd moan and complain – you see more of him than of me – because except for the mirror in the corner Archie's place felt peaceful and clean.

The mirror was tall and thin and waited for Chris to walk past. He'd turn his head so it wouldn't catch him but usually he was too slow. One night he couldn't stand it so when Archie went out to make a cuppa, Chris turned the mirror to the wall. I've tricked ya.

But next night it sat there again, gleaming like a trap or a snare. I'll fix ya, thought Chris. I'll fix ya and he turned it to a leaden-grey pane as Archie pushed open the door. You hiding? Why are you hiding? Archie was skinny but strong. You hiding? Why are you hiding? and he caught hold of Chris by the arm. You hiding? You think you don't deserve to breathe? He turned the mirror to a big silver eye and he stood there holding Chris, who could only feel his own body and the pressure of the warm hand on his neck. There's nothing wrong with you. You're a good-looking boy.

Chris heard the roar and crackle of the fire, he saw the man holding him and he ran into the soft enveloping rain. He felt the water strike his face and hoped it would wash him away and wash away what he had seen. When he reached home, he tore all his clothes off and left them in a wet pile on the floor. He lay in bed all night shivering and gasping and feeling the pressure of the warm hand on his neck.

What's the matter? Ya look like a sick bloody cat, his mother said when she came into wake him but Chris couldn't tell her. He kept seeing his face in the mirror and feeling the warm hand on his neck. It made him feel sick to his stomach, it made him feel sick to his guts. I'm not going there any more, he told her, I'm gunna stay home and help Dad.

It stayed in his mind, that hand on his neck, and night after night he lay awake thinking, until he finally cooked up a plan. There was an old peeve called Gummy who liked to hang around the toilets in town. Gummy was a bit touched, a bit simple and he'd do anything that you asked. So Chris started making up stories about Archie and what he'd asked Gummy to do. That's bullshit, the blokes in the pub said, but Chris could see the doubt in their eyes. That's bullshit, in really loud voices. He seems like a really nice bloke.

But the stories were like small fanged animals scurrying through the night, feeding and breeding in dung. Well, sometimes you can't tell, the blokes said, uneasily, shifting their hips. You can't tell, you can't tell, there's no knowing. Some of them look like you or me. Some blokes stopped talking to Archie and some of them stopped buying his stock and one evening when he was in town, he had paint thrown all over his car. A no-hoper from somewhere else, the local cop said and seemed happy to leave it at that. Archie said g'day and he gave a puzzled look when he ran into Chris in town but Chris just turned his head and looked in a window then hurriedly down at the ground.

Things might have stopped there but anyway what happened next wasn't his fault, it was the fault of that bloody psycho Andrew, home from the army on leave. Andrew didn't cry any more, he owned a big black car and the sun threw spears of light from the windscreen as he drove up the track to the house. Let's have a few beers, let's chase a few chicks, and later that night Chris told him. He left out the room and the fire and old shabby books. He touched me, was all he could say.

That old poofta! I'll teach him! I'll show him! Andrew threw a glass against the wall. He picked up a shard and shouted and left a trail of blood along the bar. All next day, he talked of nothing else; he put on mirror sunglasses and drove his big black car from house to house and his words caught the dry tinder of fear. You want to come with us? but Chris shook his head and went inside to the dog. I don't want nothin' to do with it. It's got nothin' to do with me. He went to Gwennie's place and put his head between her breasts and he didn't feel anything at all.

He didn't feel anything until the headline two days later – Local Man Hospitalised – except that it was all wrong, as the blokes in the pub said, because Archie wasn't a local at all. Got what he deserved was what most of them said; he never tried to fit in. Archie lay in hospital for nearly three weeks and when he came out he moved away. Chris never saw him again but before Andrew went back to base he told Chris about the body and the blood and Chris felt the blows and the kicks. He got excited by the body on the ground and the bright swirling patterns of blood. He paced up and down and shouted; he made the bedroom walls vibrate. Cut it out, you no-hoper, said his father, on his way out to mend the roof of his shed. He had his sleeves rolled up; Chris saw the pale brown of winter and the bark brown of summer, saw the muddy border between the two. Shut up, you old coon, you're all piss and wind.

He went past his mother and sister sitting in the kitchen with their latest pile of magazines. He walked out of the house and found Gwennie unpacking bags of lollies in the shop. I've got something new to show you, she shyly told him, as she turned around the sign on the shop door. She came back dressed like a girl in Chris's magazines except it was all half a size too small. He just looked at the black lace over fat-dimpled thighs and he started to laugh and laugh. She ran sobbing to the bathroom while all the time he sat there and laughed and laughed. It's all right, I didn't mean it, it's all right, come here. She made sounds like a rabbit in a trap as he turned her on her stomach and fucked her while the sky darkened and the rain formed black puddles on the ground.

I'm glad that he's gone, said Gwennie, when they'd finished. I'm glad that he's gone, aren't you?

Yeah, he was trouble, all right. Chris lay on his side and he watched her, the bluish veins and bloom of purple bruises around her neck. He thought about the flowers and the fire; he thought about the trampled earth, the body and the blood. He turned away and he didn't feel anything at all.

Winter Fruit

'Perhaps you could call the band "The Crass Bitches",' Ellen suggests.

Diana glances up witheringly. 'That's a really stupid idea.'

They are in the kitchen of the third-floor apartment where one of Ellen's early oils, a tiny dot of yellow in the heart of a great swathe of flame, takes up most of one wall. The apartment block is brick, vaguely art deco, and was built in the twenties. It's seen better days: there is a rambling and unkempt garden below but when Ellen looks through the kitchen window she can see the whole suburb spread out and glimpse a distant turquoise tear of ocean. She's making biscuits for Diana's birthday party, forming hearts and stars from dough using metal cutters. This is traditional: when Diana was small and Ellen was bringing her up on her own, the biscuits were a cheap and easy treat. She's kept on making them although she is now moderately successful and her paintings sell quite well. Diana's about to be fifteen but instead of going out somewhere to drink alcohol and behave raucously she's just having a few girlfriends over, including the three with whom she's forming the band. This is what has given rise to Ellen's comment: Diana has referred to one of the girls as a 'crass bitch'.

'We don't really want to call it anything that suggests that it's an all-girl band.'

'But it is.'

'Yes, but people can see that.' Diana bends over her page, scribbling. She has straight blonde hair, brown eyes and a slightly Roman nose. She's never called Di and 'handsome' is a word which will be often applied to her once she enters her thirties.

'Well, what do you want the name to say?' Ellen asks.

'It's doesn't have to say anything.'

'Then you may as well call it the Retarded Wombats.'

'You really are stupid sometimes.'

Ellen finishes cutting out the dough. She eases all the shapes onto a greased tray which she slides into the oven. Her mother taught her this recipe nearly thirty years ago; it's written down somewhere, in a round childish hand and stashed with all the others in a hall cupboard. She glances over at Diana. She doesn't understand this all-girl thing. When she was fifteen, all she thought about was boys. Is Diana on her way to becoming a lesbian? Not that Ellen would mind: not really. She has several friends who are gay. When she reminisces to Diana about her days at art school, she talks about going out to dance to the Go-Betweens or the Machinations or the Reels and being swept up in an androgynous sea of sweaty bodies. 'Fuck art, let's dance!' they used to cry at the Prince of Wales or the Seaview Ballroom. When Ellen talks about these nights, Diana looks at her the same way she would view a prehistoric animal but Ellen likes to think that it's these conversations which have made her daughter decide to learn the drums.

'Sludge said he'd help.' Diana tears off a scribbled page and starts a new one.

'Sludge plays the drums?'

'Apparently.' Ellen's not so successful that she can afford to turn down extra sources of income and she sublets the apartment's small third bedroom to a first-year uni student from Cobram. He's a quiet boy who often looks unhappy but Ellen can't tell whether this is caused by homesickness or the engineering course he's studying. She should find out, she thinks, but then all thoughts of Sludge vanishes because Diana suddenly puts down her pen.

'What happened to those other cutters? The cutters in the shape of fruit.'

Ellen's silent. After the night with Sal, she had thrown the cutters away. She couldn't bear to look at them again. She has always thought that Diana had been too young to remember. She had only been two; two and a half.

'You know the ones I mean. The cutters shaped like apples, pears and bananas.'

'Yes, I know.' Ellen turns and makes an unnecessary adjustment to the oven. Through its grease-stained window she sees the hearts and stars begin to swell and brown. She remembers the pointy-toed, lace-up boots Sal used to wear and wonders if she is still alive. She turns round and looks at her daughter. Diana stares back guilelessly. No, she doesn't remember.

'They must have got lost,' Ellen says. 'We were always moving.'

'We had them at the flat in Robe Street.'

'No, they were gone by then.'

The Robe Street flat was two addresses after the night with Sal. It had been a pinched white box but a palace compared to the place where Ellen had spent that terrible winter. She needs to change the subject.

'Keep an eye on the biscuits. I've got to get ready for Steve's opening.'

This has the required effect. Diana lets out a huge yawn; she hates the art world. 'Sham, bam, thank you mam,' she said rudely two nights ago as a sculptor and a performance artist exited the apartment. Diana intends to become a doctor.

Ellen crosses the kitchen and enters the baroque jumble of her studio with relief. Two leftover store mannequins, armless and spray-painted gold, guard the doorway and inside is the detritus of all her exploration: loops of glass beads, spirals of dried grass, a large Japanese fan, miniature torsos modelled in clay. Her sketches and drawings are tacked up all over the walls, as are reproductions of her favourite paintings. She pauses in front of Simone Martini's *Annunciation*. Underneath its helmet of gold leaf, the Virgin's face is fraught, not ready. Are any of us ever ready, thinks Ellen. She was raised with the Madonna, taught to pray to her in times of temptation. 'Yield not to temptation for yielding is sin'; 'The Devil finds work for idle hands': these had been some of Ellen's mother's favourites. She had also possessed a stock of secular truisms: 'All good things come to those who wait'; 'Sometimes you need to draw a line…'

'I draw a line,' she said, when Ellen was seventeen.

'Easier than drawing a perfect circle.' Ellen, in her final year of high school, had recently discovered thirteenth-century Italy, was entranced by Giotto and Martini, the bodies in their paintings struggling to emerge from Byzantine contortion into the clear plastic light of the Renaissance.

She had also been locked in battle with her parents about her career choice.

'Do something useful first.' Her mother had held her line.

Ellen had stayed at home and put in two years at the local library before she could get away to art school.

'Well, perhaps you could become an art teacher.'

'It's not the same as being an artist.'

Not the same, not the same: they were not the same. Ellen started drawing nudes and her mother kept drawing lines: when Ellen came home sporting a Celtic tattoo, when she moved in with Sean, when she got pregnant.

'You should get married.'

'I can't. He's pissed off to Queensland.'

The date for the abortion came and went, then came and went again. Diana was born early on a September morning. 'She's named for the huntress, not the princess,' Ellen kept explaining to the hospital staff over the next few days.

'Oh, she's perfect!' cooed Sal, her waist slung with several studded leather belts, her hair dyed midnight black and wildly spiked above kohl-rimmed eyes. She had been at art school with Ellen, was majoring in drama and dance. She and Ellen talked about how they were going to raise the baby together, talked about it as though it was some great adventure and Diana was a soft squashy toy, Ellen thinks, as she pins a sheet of butcher's paper to the easel in the corner.

They had managed all right for a while. They had been lucky.

Diana was a placid baby who slept through classes and didn't get sick. Ellen finished her course, didn't enrol for a diploma of education, kept painting. Her mother kept sending money which Ellen returned. She and Sal and Diana weathered the first winter in a cheap but spacious flat not far from the art school. But then…they had to move out of the flat and couldn't find anywhere which would take a toddler. Ellen had ended up in a bleak and draughty half-house without furniture. She lost her waitressing job. Sal, always fond of party drugs, started experimenting with heroin; Ellen, cold, exhausted, too poor to paint, joined in.

'The biscuits are nearly done, Mum!'

'Well, take them out if they're ready.'

Ellen selects a thick, soft-leaded pencil then marks the paper with several broad slashing lines. She closes her eyes for a moment and sees Sal in the dismal kitchen on a day in July when the sun burned a distant white hole in the sky. She sees the spoon, the flame, the hypo, the child in the background. During the next couple of days she heard it crying, seems to remember that she got up and did things to it but she was locked inside the silver delirium of junk, swimming far down on tides dictated by blood craving. On the morning of the third day, she surfaced to find Diana on the floor next to her, rocking unsteadily on her legs after escaping from the cot.

'We've got to get some more stuff,' said Sal.

'What about her?'

'Feed her, then we'll go out.'

There was no food in the house except a few spoonfuls of flour, a little sugar and a single egg. There was no milk – Ellen had used water to make a paste – and no butter. She rummaged in the drawer to find the fruit-shaped cutters. 'Winter fruit, winter fruit,' she crooned, as she mixed the thin dough. 'This is winter fruit, Di-sy.' After the biscuits hardened into pale wafers in the oven, she put them in a bowl which she placed in the cot. She tied Diana to its bars with the sash from an old dressing gown. Then she went to the Prince of Wales with Sal.

In the kitchen the phone rings and Ellen hears her daughter punctuating dialogue with giggles. She remembers similar conversations when she was Diana's age and she was marooned on the farm. She stares at the paper before her and adds some more lines: two eyes above a full-lipped mouth gaze back. The merchant seaman she and Sal met in the public bar of the Prince of Wales had lips like that, wet and slightly loose. Very red. Looking back, Ellen realises that he must have known what they were, he must have been watching them. That's what he told them when he came up to the bar. 'I like to watch. My name is Grigor. You can call me Greg.'

Sal had tried to haggle but he saw the demon-need glowing in her eyes. 'I can find it somewhere else. I just want to watch.' Ellen was still spacey from the drug: when she followed them to one of the rooms above the pub she wasn't aware of feeling anything although she seemed to know what to do. Her tongue and hands moved over Sal's body while her mind floated up to the ceiling and stayed there, looking down, watching as she circled Sal's nipples and then parted her legs. She hadn't been frightened, although she was aware of a grunting presence behind her, a dark shape on the edge of her vision.

After she and Sal dressed, he brought out a bottle. 'Drink! Drink! We must all drink!'

The scald of vodka made the room spin and blurred the ugly blue and pink flowers patterning the sofa. As she passed out, Ellen saw the sailor reaching for Sal.

She woke in the hour which separates the night people going home and the day people standing in line for trams. She lay there feeling groggy and sick; then she remembered. She fell off the sofa and crawled across the room. She left the snoring huddles on the bed and ran through a city spread with sticky red light. It glazed the doors of shabby rooming houses and milk bar windows as a yammering incantation, please, please, please, leapt through her, joining with futile promises to futile gods. By the time she reached the house, she was moaning and crying; as she opened the door, she bent over to vomit.

She didn't know what she expected to find but Diana lay asleep in her cot, soiled but quite unharmed. Most of the biscuits were gone. She waved her arms and made pre-verbal grizzles as Ellen untied and changed her. It was very cold in the flat and Ellen took her coat off and placed it on top of the blankets when she crawled underneath them with her child. They fell asleep curled together and when she woke she lay listening to the quiet breathing. I'll die if I go on like this. She took the money the sailor had given her to the supermarket then went home and composed a long grovelling letter. 'Well, it's about time you saw sense,' came the reply. The cheques arrived regularly until Ellen found her feet. When her mother died some years later, she also left Ellen some money, not a fortune, but enough to pay for Diana's education.

'You keep it,' Ellen told her brother. 'You keep it. I don't need it.' It was perverse, she knew, but enough was enough. She drew a line. She drew one with Sal as well. After the night at the Prince of Wales, they met a couple of times, awkwardly, and during the next few months Ellen occasionally saw her walking along Barkly Street, the wind whipping her thighs or standing on one of the Grey Street corners, talking to men. Whenever this happened, Ellen crossed the street. With the money from the first cheque, she bought and stretched a large canvas then covered it with a liquid spill of vermilion. Yellow she chose for its ambivalence: energy, optimism and the heat of the sun, as well as cowardice, betrayal and madness. She thought about calling the finished painting *Self portrait* but decided this was self-indulgent so left it untitled.

She kept on making the biscuits, both as a reminder and a promise.

Ellen stands back and regards her finished sketch. It's a face seamed and coarsened by time, not a face she's ever seen before but belonging to someone she might once have known. Her gaze wanders across the wall to a reproduction of Hugo van der Goes' *Adoration of the Magi* where the radiant Child nestles among cooing angels and flowers. The boys made it look so easy; you had to search hard to get the real picture. There's a birth image by a Pintubi woman on the same wall. The baby looks as though it's being shat out of the mother.

'The biscuits are burning, Mum!' Ellen sprints to the kitchen to save them. 'Nice and crunchy.' She leaves them on the bench to cool then bends to kiss her daughter.

'You are my morning star.'

'Yeah, I know.'

A pile of schoolbooks now sits beside Diana's right elbow. Her page is covered with drawings of aliens and mutant space creatures. Strange animals with bat wings and glaring faces take off into the stratosphere.

'Don't stay up too late.' Ellen heads for the shower then dresses carefully in linen and brightly-patterned silk.

On her way out, she meets her boarder coming up the stairs. 'Hi, Gavin,' she says, which is Sludge's real name.

He mumbles a greeting and moves shyly past. Ellen steps into a day where the sun is a benign yellow orb and fat pigeons scavenge. People sit chatting at tables outside cafés and there's the cheerful clatter of trendy commerce from bookshops and clothes shops. A few blocks from the gallery she has to get off the footpath and walk around scaffolding and holes in the ground. The Prince of Wales is being renovated into a series of moodily lit bars for its new clientele of media executives and marketing consultants. The old landscape of her memory has gradually been obliterated and the suburb's become as sleek and presentable as herself, although at night transsexual whores cruise the side streets, standing silent and hostile beneath the gaze of plain clothes police who drive past slowly.

Ellen doesn't waste time on any of this. She is looking forward to the opening, with its attendant bitchiness and ego-tripping, and to seeing Anton, an old friend, married but with whom she enjoys the occasional companionable bonk. Her own last show sold out; she's on her way to being famous. 'All good things come to those who wait.' No: sometimes you walk through fire and come out the other side.

Portraits from the First Republic

Der Schöner Geist, Vienna, 1927

The day after her mother dies, Gretel runs away from home. She packs a small portmanteau and, when the maid is not looking, lets herself out the front door. Spring flowers crowd the garden. White jasmine and roses drown her in scent; for a moment, she thinks she will vomit. She has taken money from the pocket of one of her father's suits and stolen what has been left out for Teresa to do the shopping. It's enough to sustain her for two or three days. She does not think beyond that time. The dark-leaved street, with its spacious houses and sedate tiers of apartments, is quiet as she walks along it, stopping now and again to put down the suitcase.

Gretel carries no map of the city except the one in her head and that's sketchy and selective: the streets she knows contain department stores, the convent and the homes of her parents' friends. This was the city of her childhood. Now she wants something else. She walks along the Ringstrasse, the great promenade built last century after the city's medieval fortifications were torn down. Massive statues of dead Habsburg rulers glare down at passers-by, as though daring them to forget the glory of their empire, so recently surrendered, so irretrievably gone.

Cafe Kaos is not on the Ringstrasse; it's too shabby, too louche, for that. Gretel turns down a side street then another. She crosses a small footbridge and glimpses her reflection in grey water darker than the sky. Outside the café a black dog sits and scratches. Scabs of paint flake from the door. No matter: Hilde has told Gretel that this is where you find artists and writers. She would be disappointed if the place was neat.

She enters the café and is immediately impaled by several dozen eyes. There is a soft male laugh and a whispered comment, '*Knochig Arsch.*' Gretel flushes but stands her ground. She chooses a centre table. As she sits down, the waiter catches her eye then returns to his conversation with the barman.

Gretel glances about. The opposite wall is a montage of photos showing celebrity patrons, past and present. Gretel recognises Picasso and Tristan Tzara, Josephine Baker and Hannah Hoch. There are racks of newspapers, in French and English as well as German, and some in languages at which she can only guess: Russian, Yiddish. Hastily she plucks the nearest paper – it's the *Arbeiter Zeitung* – and turns the pages slowly.

She reads about striking mine workers in Styria. There's been another violent clash at the university between Socialists and Heimwahr supporters: three students are in hospital. A new housing cooperative has opened in the working-class district of Vienna. A photo shows a smiling woman and child standing in a tiny front garden. Briefly, the black and white pages blur before Gretel's eyes then the type recomposes. Her mind crowds with memories of family holidays and Christmases (the tree always topped with a shining Star of David.)

She undoes the suitcase and takes out the camera. She places it on the table as the waiter finally approaches.

'Yes, miss?'

Gretel orders black coffee. When it arrives, she sips and turns the pages of another paper. At places like this, you're able to stay for several hours, slowly sipping one coffee. She plans to stay for as long as she can. She tries not to think about the night ahead.

'You like pictures?' A man and a woman, who have been leaning against the wall watching her ever since she came in, sit down at Gretel's table.

The woman wears a dress of synthetic black stuff. She looks at Gretel from pale eyes cored by pinprick pupils. The man is in his mid-thirties. His jacket is shiny but his hair isn't and one of his front teeth has broken off.

He gestures to the camera. 'You like pictures, eh?'

Gretel ignores him. In the circles in which she has been raised, this would suffice but this man, with his unmanicured fingernails and Eastern European accent, is not from those circles.

'You like dirty pictures?' He stares at her. 'You like dirty pictures, nude pictures?'

The woman giggles. She leans against his shoulder and chews a thumbnail. Gretel glimpses the outline of a tattoo, smudgy and violent as a bruise, at the neckline of the dress. The man takes something from his coat and passes it to Gretel, who averts her eyes although she knows about the sex act. Hilde has told her what happens. She wishes Hilde were here. Hilde would know what to do.

Just as Gretel is planning to rise and retreat with minimal loss of dignity, a man approaches the table. Gretel recognises the famous Journalist. He used to live in Vienna but then the paper for which he wrote folded so he moved to Berlin. Now he lives in Paris and writes novels. He's in one of the photographs on the wall, part of a laughing group which features members of the Yiddish Theatre.

'Scram, Ivan, and take your putain with you.'

The man opens his mouth but he sees the barman watching. Without a word, he and the woman resume their place at the wall.

The Journalist pulls out a chair and regards Gretel unsmilingly. 'You shouldn't be here. This is no place for nice, middle-class little girls like you. Go home.'

Gretel is annoyed. She has had enough. She points the camera across the table and takes his photo.

The Journalist laughs. 'Oh, ho! Who have we here? The next Madame d'Ora?'

Gretel flushes again. (She has vivid memories of being taken to that lady's atelier as an eight-year-old, wearing a white ruffled dress from beneath which peeked lacy pantalettes. There had been hours of fussing, the woman posing her this way and that while the studio assistant huddled, muttering, under the camera dark cloth.)

'Of course not. Her photos are…sentimental.'

The Journalist laughs again. Now that Gretel looks at him closely, she sees red veins, fine as the by-way markings on maps, riddling his cheeks and nose. It's mid-afternoon but his eyes and hands say much later.

'How old are you? Fifteen?'

'Seventeen.'

'Where are your parents?'

'My mother's dead,' Gretel says abruptly. (The summer before last she started to cough. She held a lace-edged handkerchief to her mouth and turned her head away. 'It's nothing, *liebchen*, just a little cold,' but by winter the cough was worse and red roses bloomed on the snowy lawn.)

'Ah, yes, it's hard when your parents leave.' He looks at her sympathetically. 'My own parents…well, I left them, actually…'

'How old were you?' Gretel looks at him intently. She wants to hear about his travels, find out about his experiences during the war and learn how he became a writer. She wants to know everything.

The Journalist tells her. Gretel journeys with him from Eastern Poland to the Western Front then shares his hunger and loneliness after he demobilises. 'I had to earn my living somehow so I thought I'd try scribbling…'

He breaks off and gazes intently over Gretel's right shoulder. A strange expression comes over his face; yearning but with a touch of brutality beneath. Gretel turns her head. She sees Hilde, wearing a dress of pale pink crêpe-de-chine, crossing the café. Light from the one dusty window strikes her waist-length red-gold hair looped carelessly at the nape of her neck and, for a moment, she's crowned with a fiery halo. As she passes, some conversations falter; others cease completely.

Hilde is unfazed. Since she was twelve, boys and their fathers have been turning to stare at her in the street. This man at the table, on the brink of middle age, is no different. She walks straight up to Gretel and inclines her head like the minor aristocrat she actually is. 'Your father's worried. Come home.'

'Won't you sit down?' The Journalist springs to his feet. He pulls out a chair for Hilde. 'Would you like a coffee? Perhaps a lemonade?'

Gretel wants to laugh. She has seen all this before. Later, Hilde will shrug and say, 'Men are so predictable. They're simple as children, really.' Now, she merely inclines her head again. 'I'm sorry. We must go.'

'Oh, please…' The Journalist is almost pleading.

Gretel remembers gossip she has heard. The Journalist has his own sorrow. His wife is in an asylum. He has many lovers but a broken heart.

'Well…' Hilde sits down and her presence makes a party.

The Journalist orders coffee, lemonade and a plate of cream cakes. (The icing is garish and congealed but no one cares.) The Journalist plies them both with questions: he asks them about their aspirations once they finish at the convent. They ask him about the novel he is writing.

He listens to Gretel but his eyes never leave Hilde's Raphaelite Madonna face. 'You're not thinking of becoming a nun, are you? That would be a terrible waste.'

Hilde looks demure. 'A true vocation is a gift from God.'

The Journalist makes a rude sound then leans forward slightly. 'Will I see you again?'

'I'm sure Mama and Papa wouldn't like me coming to places like this. Who knows what might happen?'

'Oh, is that what you're worried about?' The Journalist crosses the café and for several minutes speaks to the barman. who nods briefly as he polishes a glass. When the Journalist resumes his seat. he beams at them both. 'There, I've fixed it. You're under my protection. No harm will come to you here. Now, before you go, let's all have a liqueur.'

When Gretel emerges onto the street a little later. the world is unfocused and fuzzy at the edges. Beside her, Hilde laughs, infatuated with her own success. She takes Gretel's arm but, for the first time in their three-year friendship, Gretel shakes her off. She needs to get home. She has so much to think about. She struggles along with the suitcase, the camera dangling from her shoulder by its leather strap. Already it feels necessary, like a part of her.

Two days later, she goes to the cathedral. Her mother was denied a wedding here because she was marrying a Jew but an early death from tuberculosis is a different matter. She lies in a coffin wearing a white dress, surrounded by lilies. Her face is alabaster, white as bone, but her lips have been subtly rouged, giving her a sophistication which is unearthly, slightly macabre. She looks like a beautiful ghost, like a woman in a Gustav Klimt painting. Gretel stares at her for a moment. She takes out the camera and frames the scene. Her mother will putrefy. Her flesh will rot and fall away. 'My mother's dead.' When she said those words the event became real to her. It began to pass into history. This photo will be past tense too. Past tense but present; like holding a ghost in your hand. Gretel knows she cannot defeat time. You try to freeze a fraction of a second but it rushes on, regardless. No matter. Her magic futile quest stretches before her. She presses the shutter.

Der Adler, Vienna, 1928

Gretel turns herself into an eagle. She turns into a moving eye. She moves ever deeper into this city she seeks to know. The camera takes her there.

She sees the textile worker, face gaunt and body heavy from children, on her way to her twelve-hour shift. She sees the seamstress rising before dawn, eyes made blind by her flashing needle. Gretel stops thinking these people are there to serve her. She sees that they have no choice. She stops thinking she is special. She sees that she is merely lucky. She sees hunger. She sees illness without cure. She sees people who have only themselves to sell.

They are not always happy to be Gretel's subjects. Sometimes they curse her or throw stones. Twice she is pursued by shouting men wanting her camera and money. Gretel takes it all back with her, distilling this violence in the eerie red light of the dark room. (Teresa complains about the chemical smell but there's nothing she can do.)

The nuns speak to that nice Herr Doktor Mendelssohn about his daughter's intermittent attendance at school. They hint at a lack of feminine influence in the home. Perhaps dancing lessons and introductions to young men… Herr Mendelssohn calls in his older sister, who takes Gretel to a fashionable salon. Gretel wants watered black silk which bares her shoulders, but this is ruled out as unsuitable. A white dress is chosen, something appropriate for a young lady's first formal dance. Gretel lays it on the bed and cuts it to ribbons. She takes her camera and goes back to the streets.

Two old men play chess in a sunlit park. How can they say no to this smiling girl with the amusing toy? When she returns with prints the following week, one man gives her money. Gretel uses it to have her hair cut off. The black tresses coil like dead snakes then kiss the floor. She shakes her head in relief.

On the morning of her sixteenth birthday, her father appears with a square gift-wrapped box in his hands. It's a new Leica, the best camera on the market. It's small and fast and quiet, the perfect predator's tool.

Gretel thanks him, not meeting his eyes. 'Will you let me go to art school?'

'You must promise to be a good girl. Work hard for the sisters. Then we'll see.' He regards her sadly for a moment. 'Ah, Gretchen, you used to have such pretty hair.'

Gretel ignores him. (She cannot enter his river of grief. She will drown.) She opens the curtains then props the camera on top of the bookcase and stands before it. Light slashes her face. The print shows her gazing rapt, visionary, eyes aflame like a saint's. Gretel pins it to the wall. Only the image is pure. She distrusts all words. Only the image speaks. She takes the new camera and goes back to the streets. She tells no one about what she sees except the Journalist; and Hilde, who has commenced her own strange and difficult journey.

'Only the image is pure,' she tells the Journalist when she meets him at Cafe Kaos the week after her birthday.

'Oh, you think so, do you?' he mutters. His hand shakes slightly as he sets down a fresh glass of schnapps then looks at her quizzically. 'The next time you come here, I'll show you something. Bring your friend.'

Gretel does not bring Hilde. (Hilde has lost all interest in places like Cafe Kaos.) She orders a coffee and sits at the table until the Journalist arrives. Without a word, he throws down a yellowing copy of *Der Neue Tag*, dated 1920.

Gretel peers at the slightly smudgy image on the front page. 'It's Lenin.'

'Very good. You certainly are a very smart girl.'

Gretel curses him under her breath. She looks at the photo of the dead revolutionary leaning across a dais to address crowds of soldiers below. She spots two vaguely familiar figures at the foot of the dais. 'There's Trotsky and…someone else…'

'Lev Kamenev – he hasn't been driven into exile like Trotsky, just driven out of the Communist Party.'

'So?' Gretel looks up and frowns.

The Journalist places another paper of top. It's Russian, *Pravda*, and it's dated last week. She sees the same photo.

'They're gone!'

'That's right. Comrade Stalin has decided that history can do without Comrade Trotsky. If I were Comrade Kamenev, I'd be very nervous.'

Gretel shrugs. The power struggles in the Soviet Union mean nothing to her. However, she looks with interest at the two photos and this new possibility.

'Of course,' the Journalist continues, 'we both know that Comrade Stalin's no friend of the Jews and Trotsky and Kamenev are both…'

'Oh!' Now Gretel is annoyed. 'It's just politics, nothing more.' She repeats what her father has said to her, more than once: 'You mustn't see prejudice where there is none.'

'And what would you know about prejudice, little one?'

'Oh, I don't know why I talk to you!'

He smiles at her. 'It's because I'm a genius – and women are drawn to genius.'

'I'm not Alma Mahler,' Gretel snaps. She stands up, almost upsetting the table, then walks out with the sound of his laughter behind her.

On her way home, Gretel does something she has never done before. She seeks out the synagogue which her father still occasionally attends and stands outside. It's Saturday. Afternoon sunlight strikes shards of coloured light from the Star of David above the main door. She hears the swell of organ and choir beneath the clear soaring tenor. 'Hear, O Israel, hear, the Lord your God is King…' The sound rolls over her as though it will never end.

Der schöner Akt, Vienna, 1929

The heavy studio camera is still foreign to Gretel. She wheels it across the floor, almost tipping it over as it tangles in a coil of electrical leads.

'Do be careful, cherie,' Hilde purrs, as she reclines against the black velvet backdrop. Apart from a large ring set with semi-precious stones, she is completely naked. 'You break something, they'll know it was you.'

'I am being careful.' Gretel rights the camera, positions it in front of the low dais then struggles with the knobs which control the bellows apparatus. She barely looks at Hilde, whose nudity is new. (The nuns discouraged such behaviour.) Gretel walks around the studio collecting several lights. She feels out of place, like a tiger in a cage at a zoo or a wild flower in a hot house. This was all Hilde's idea.

Hilde is completely relaxed. She lies back against several large cushions, her red-gold hair cascading over white flesh marbled with rose. Next to her, Gretel feels ugly and dark.

'She wants the photos as a six-month anniversary present for Pauli,' Gretel told the Journalist in Cafe Kaos yesterday.

'Oh, really?' He had been doodling absent-mindedly on a table napkin while they talked but, at the mention of Hilde's name, put the pen down. 'This Pauli – she's pretty?'

'Well…'

By day, Pauli took tickets from commuters on the tramcars which criss-crossed Vienna. By night, she wore a collar and a tie and called herself Paul. (Once, a girl like Hilde would never have met a girl like Pauli but things have changed for Hilde's family.)

Gretel considered. Pauli was 'striking', perhaps. 'Pretty', never. 'She's handsome.'

The Journalist gave a theatrical shudder. He took her hand and played with it meditatively, across the table. 'I suppose she wears a collar and tie and calls herself Paul. I suppose she has short hair.'

Gretel laughed. She had never met anyone who knew people the way he did, who could skewer their psychology so mercilessly.

'They met in a bar. You go up some stairs to a black metal door…'

'I'm sure. I know what such places are like.' He looked at his watch. 'I must go. I'm meeting a publisher in half an hour.' He put money on the table and walked away.

Gretel lightly touched her fingertips to where his had been. All day she did this, as though to rekindle the warmth of that pressure.

Gretel sets up the lights. It is then, and only then, that she notices that just below her navel, Hilde has a large splotch of darker tissue. It's round and slightly raised, like a lesion or something more primeval. On Hilde, it's like seeing a sixth finger or webbed feet. Gretel shivers then concentrates on gilding the flesh before her.

'Pauli wants something romantic,' Hilde murmurs. She rearranges herself against the cushions and leans back with her arms pillowing her head.

'Keep still!' snaps Gretel. She rearranges the lights to reduce contrast. She adjusts the depth of field so that a shoulder and a thigh soften. Since she took her first photos, she has learned a lot, about technique and about photographic history. She refuses to produce anything as gauzy and sentimental as the images of the Pictorialists but she will print these negatives on a warm-toned paper then immerse them in a sepia bath. If Pauli wants romantic, then she shall have romantic.

Gretel makes several exposures then several more. These last few are different: harder, the definition so sharp that you can see the crease beneath the glowing bushy pudenda.

Hilde fidgets. 'I'm cold. This is boring.'

'Almost done.' Gretel uses the soothing but detached tone of a doctor to a patient. She takes a final image, a portrait. Hilde's head lolls against the pillow, her lips parted and her eyes unfocused, gazing from the frame. While she dresses, Gretel packs away the camera and lights with relief; her hands long for the Leica. She and Hilde clatter down the stairs and burst out into the afternoon. They link arms and walk along the Ringstrasse singing,

The tenth man, he's a charmer, the tenth man, he can't be caught.
The tenth man he gives me many kisses then he leaves me silent as a dream…

When Gretel sees a group of strolling young army officers approach, she tenses and wants to cross the street. Recently, on the way to Cafe Kaos, two such men followed her, calling her 'Jew bitch' and 'Red whore'. However, this group are all smiles. One of them, his face marked with ritual duelling scars, bows deeply in Hilde's direction.

'That's Franz,' Hilde murmurs. 'His father was an intimate of Emperor Franz Joseph, and his family still own much land. My parents…' She sighs and is silent.

It's spring time again. Ice melts on the mountains and birds sing in the Vienna Woods as the trees unfurl their first spikes of green.

Gretel makes the first batch of prints and hangs them up to dry. They've turned out better than she hoped. She smiles. 'Turned out': it sounds as though she has been baking a cake. She slides the prints into the sepia bath and watches the dark tones alchemise to golden-brown. The mark below Hilde's navel is visible but Pauli won't mind. She is liebeskrank, lovesick. Now she has a true image of her beloved. Gretel lays the prints aside and turns to her second project.

She takes a negative – it's one that is sharply focused – and places it in the enlarger. She cuts a tiny piece of cardboard trying to fit its shape as closely to the shape of the blemish as possible. Then when she exposes the paper beneath the enlarger light, she holds the cardboard above the disfigurement.

This is tricky and it takes her a while to get it right. Several times, Hilde comes out of the fixer with a white crater in her pelvis. Finally, however, she emerges perfect as a Titian goddess, without mark or stain. No one will be able to tell what Gretel has done when he looks at the print.

Gretel takes the tramcar across town. All the way to her destination she pitches between excitement and fear; for a moment, she thinks she will vomit. She gazes out the window and breathes slowly, taking in the landscape. A cinema writes Greta Garbo's name in neon. A theatre proclaims Claire Bauroff the greatest dancer of the day. Far above, glimpsed for a blurred second, a woman wearing slinky black advertises playing cards.

After a few minutes, Gretel is calmer. Rejection will make her feel a fool; that's the worst that can happen. That's all. She alights from the tramcar and looks for the apartment block he has mentioned several times.

He answers her knock with the familiar ironic gleam in his eye. 'Aha! My protégé, my spiritual child, my wild eagle winging her way through the storm… Come in. I'll make coffee.'

Gretel has expected semi-squalor, faded wallpaper and overflowing ashtrays but over his shoulder she sees that the place is spacious, airy, even chic, with blonde wood furniture and a low chrome table. Further back, the bed beckons.

She hands him the paper envelope. 'Let me show you something,' she says.

www.ingramcontent.com/pod-product-compliance
Lightning Source LLC
Chambersburg PA
CBHW030211130726
47898CB00012B/977

9 781760 417130